“Interview With A Master

Jason Luke

She was smiling, and there was something smug and self-satisfied about the expression that pissed me off. She had no right to be smiling, and she certainly had no right to be satisfied.

"Is that it, then?" I asked flatly. "Is that all you want to know?"

The woman set down her pen, leafed back through her notebook, and then looked up at me. She looked relieved.

"I think so..." she said carefully. She sat back in the chair and crossed her legs. "Unless there is more you want to tell me."

I stared at a spot on the wall an inch over her head.

More I want to tell? Fuck, the questions she had asked were the kind of questions I would expect a child to ask, not a journalist.

"Mr. Noble...?"

"Huh?"

The woman was watching me, suddenly curious. Her eyebrows were knitted together, her expression anxious and uncertain.

She was wearing a loose-fitting open-necked red sweater. She was tall, with the figure of a girl who swam, or maybe played tennis.

She had short blonde hair, the tips seemingly bleached, which again made me think she might be a swimmer. She had a nose that wasn't too large and below it, her mouth was twisted, her bottom lip trapped between her teeth in consternation. She wasn't wearing any makeup. Her lips were pink – the color of coral – and there was a soft dusting of freckles across her nose.

She brushed a tendril of hair from her face and tucked it behind her ear. It was a distinctly nervous gesture that matched perfectly with the wide-eyed expression in her eyes.

"Is there more about your BDSM lifestyle my readers should know – or is there more about your background…?"

I sat forward on the sofa and sighed. "Miss. Fall, the questions you've asked me were superficial and quite frankly immature. I don't know what I've told you in the last thirty minutes, but whatever it was, it was the same thing I've told a thousand other journalists over the past five years. You didn't need to interview me for the information you got – you just had to read what everyone else has written."

The woman blanched. She blinked her eyes and the smile slid from her lips.

Good.

"I beg your pardon…?" she asked softly.

I stood up. Thrust my hands into my pockets. "You heard me," I said. "While you've been asking your idiotic questions, I've been thinking about you. It's the only reason you're still here. Because I haven't quite made up my mind about you yet."

I started to pace across the room. I reached the side table near the door and lit a cigarette.

She followed me with her eyes. She was scowling.

"Made up your mind about what?" she asked.

I exhaled a feather of blue smoke at the ceiling. "Whether you're wearing lingerie," I said honestly. "I still haven't decided." I saw her blink, and then a sudden flush of color spread across her cheeks and neck. "And what you would look like with a submissive's leather collar around your neck."

I ashed the cigarette and turned to the window for a second. Outside, the afternoon light was fading quickly. I could see distant car headlights winding their way along the mountain road. I turned back, frowning. "With some women, you can just tell – you know instantly whether they like to be dominated, or not. As for you...? Well I'm still not sure."

There was a long, stunned silence in the room.

Fuck it. I like silence.

The woman got to her feet and snatched at her notebook. She stuffed it into her handbag and ran her splayed fingers down the length of her thigh to smooth out her skirt. She was angry now, not embarrassed. Maybe even outraged. She was making rapid little panting sounds like she was having a hard time controlling her breathing.

"Mr. Noble, I resent your language," she said stiffly. It sounded like something she might have been told to say at a sexual harassment in the workplace course.

I shrugged. "I don't care," I said – and I didn't. "The door is right there, Miss. Fall. You can walk out right now for all I care, or you can sit back down and we can do a proper interview."

She paused, like a deer suddenly caught in the headlights. "Proper?" she asked suspiciously. "What do you mean? Exactly?"

I came across the room – three quick strides so that I was standing close to her. Close enough to smell her cheap perfume and see the discomfort and panic beginning to rise in her eyes. I stared, neither of us speaking or moving for several seconds.

She was taller than I had initially thought, her head above the level of my shoulder with long sculpted legs beneath a sensible skirt that brushed across the tops of her knees. She had a small narrow waist, and the shape of her breasts beneath the loose fabric of her sweater was an ample promise.

I studied her more closely. She wasn't a child, she was a mature woman in her mid-twenties, and behind the eager nervousness of her I sensed there was an underlying resolve.

I changed my mind. She wasn't ordinary. She was attractive, but not in the obvious way I was accustomed to. Her beauty was much more subtle – like a gentle scent that lingered and took time to appreciate.

"I mean an interview like you've never had before," I promised. "An interview that no one has ever had before. I mean the works, Miss. Fall. You can ask me any question you want, and I will give you the honest truth. Any question at all." I said it again, to make sure she understood that I was offering her the opportunity of an ambitious young journalist's lifetime.

A career-making interview with America's elusive, notorious BDSM Master, Jonah Noble.

I saw the instant the realization struck her. It showed as a flicker behind her eyes – a dazzling split-second of understanding.

"And in return?" she asked me softly, and there was wary caution in her voice.

"Simple," I said. I reached out for her then. My hand cupped under the soft smooth skin of her chin. It was a distinctly intimate gesture, presumptuous and possessive, but I'm often like that with women. Her breath hitched in her throat and I felt her whole body begin to tremble.

I stared into her eyes and smiled. It was one of my better efforts – one of my slow, sexy smiles that starts at the corners of my mouth and spreads slowly across my face until it sparkles in my eyes.

"In return, you will answer the questions I have about you," I said, still holding the smile, still staring into her eyes. "For everything I tell you, you must tell me something about yourself – an exchange of secrets and information."

She went stiff. Her back straightened. "That's not fair," she said.

The smile stayed fixed on my lips. "I think it is," I countered comfortably. "After all, you still have the advantage, Miss. Fall. You can publish my story. I merely get to know yours."

* * *

"How old were you when you first became interested in BDSM?" Leticia asked me.

We had moved into the study. The walls were dark wooden panels hung with old seascapes, the drapes heavy velvet. The chairs and sofa were all upholstered in hand-crafted leather, and over the polished wooden floorboards were deep-piled

Persian rugs. It was getting dark. I lit a fire and spent a long time staring into the flickering flames, while the warm orange glow lit the walls and filled the room with leaping shadows. I considered the question for a long time.

"Can I call you Leticia?"

"Sure," the woman said, still guarded. "Can I call you Jonah? Or do you prefer to be called Master Jonah?" There was a hint of challenge in the way she asked. I ignored it.

"You can call me Jonah," I said. "If you were my submissive, you would call me Master. If you were a submissive, but not under my care and protection, you would call me Sir."

"Is that some kind of a BDSM rule?"

"It's my rule."

She made a note of that. She scribbled for a few moments into her notebook and then looked up at me expectantly. "Okay... Jonah.... So back to the original question. How old were you when you first realized you were interested in being a BDSM Master?"

I got up and started to pace. I do that a lot. I do it when I'm dictating letters to my secretary too. It's just the way I organize my thoughts, I guess. I stared down into the comforting warm glow of the fire and then turned suddenly.

I knew where I should start.

"When I was eighteen, I was in a car accident," I said. "It was pretty bad. I was a passenger in a vehicle. One of my buddies was driving. We were stopped at a set of traffic lights. The driver of the truck behind us must have fallen asleep at the wheel. He crashed into the back of our car. My friend was killed instantly, and I was hurled through the windshield. I landed on the road, twenty feet clear of the car in the middle of the intersection – or so I'm told. I don't remember anything of the crash. I was in a coma for over twelve months."

The woman gaped at me. "Twelve months?"

I nodded. "And then another six months of rehab before I was discharged from the hospital."

She wasn't making notes. She was staring up at my silhouette, framed against the firelight.

"My father was one of the wealthiest men in America. After my mother died, he devoted himself to his business and made a fortune. So when I went home from hospital, he arranged for me to have a live-in tutor. I was a long way behind in studies, and my father had ambitions of me studying law. The tutor was a woman."

Leticia made a face of slow realization. "Was this woman your first sexual encounter?"

I shook my head. "No," I said. "But she was my first serious encounter."

"And you knew instantly with this woman tutor that you were naturally interested in BDSM?" Her tone was incredulous. "At the age of nineteen?"

I laughed. The sound of it rang out in the gloomy room and seemed to echo off the walls. "No," I admitted. "I had no idea about BDSM, and not much of an idea about sex in general. I learned a lot from that woman – but initially the lessons I learned were ones of submission."

There was a long pause. I could see Leticia's expression change from understanding to puzzled confusion. She shook her head and frowned. "I don't think I follow."

I spelled it out.

"My first introduction to a sexual BDSM relationship was as a reluctant submissive to an older woman."

I started to pace again, eyes down, hands buried deep into my pockets, footsteps muffled by the deep carpet as I sifted through my memories, the images still clear and fresh in my mind after almost sixteen years.

"Her name was Claire Moreland," I said. "She was twenty-six when we met. She moved into a one-bedroom guesthouse on the grounds of my father's estate. She said she was divorced. She had long red hair, and the most amazing green eyes. When she stared at me, it was like she could see right through to my soul."

Leticia raised an eyebrow, but said nothing, and I went on quickly, the memories tumbling in my mind, each one like a clip of footage played on a screen.

"We didn't get along initially," I explained. "She was a tough woman, and she was serious about her tutoring work. I, on the other hand, was a nineteen-year-old young man. All I could think about was her; the way she walked, the purring sound of her voice, the aroma of her perfume when she leaned close to me, and the press of her breasts against her blouse. Each time she leaned over me to see what I was working on, I would feel the warmth of her thigh brush against my side. It drove me to utter distraction – and I'm quite sure she knew what she was doing."

"Really?"

I nodded. "Claire was a very unique woman," I said abstractly. "I didn't understand at first, because I was young and naïve, but she had a fierce perverse sexual energy that began to reveal itself after she caught me."

"Caught you? Caught you doing what?"

I smiled ruefully. "Spying on her."

Leticia Fall almost laughed. I could see it in her eyes and the touch of a grin at the corner of her lips. And I suppose – now – it was funny. But at the time...

"Claire had been living on the estate for about three weeks," I explained. "And every day we studied together until midafternoon. When study was finished for the day, her time was her own. We had a pool on the grounds, and she often swam laps while I was off learning boxing and martial arts."

Leticia interrupted me. "You learned martial arts?"

I frowned. A cold gust of annoyance stirred my temper. "Yes," I said curtly. "And boxing. It was part of my rehab – but it's not part of the story."

"Sorry."

I took a deep breath. I hate being interrupted.

"One day I cut martial arts classes and came back home early. I could hear Claire outside. She was swimming, and I went to the kitchen window and watched her for a long time. She was wearing a tiny bikini and she was stunning – she had a sensational figure; her breasts fascinated me. I couldn't take my eyes off them – the shape, and the way they pressed together and glistened and heaved each time she came up for breath. I was in lust! I watched her swim half a dozen laps and then I went out through the side entrance of the house and skirted the gardens. I went to the guesthouse. I had a key. I let myself in and went to the bathroom. She had three shelves stacked with lotions and potions – women's cosmetics. I'm sure you know the kind of things I'm talking about."

Leticia nodded.

I stopped for a moment and smiled contritely. "I drilled a peep hole through her bathroom wall," I confessed. "And then disguised it behind some bottles of cosmetics. There was a bushy garden alongside the building. I went out and crouched in the shadows, and waited for her to finish swimming."

Leticia was following me with her eyes as I moved around the room. I returned to the fireplace and stood there for a moment, lost in thought until I heard her clear her throat discreetly. When I turned around she was looking up at me with her pen poised over her notepad and a curious expectant expression on her face. Not one of approval, but one of intrigue.

"And she caught you?"

I shook my head. "No. Not the first time. But the next afternoon, when I went back to the garden and waited for her to finish her laps, I was surprised. She normally swam for an hour. This day, she was back, standing wet in her bathroom with a towel wrapped around her, not thirty minutes after we had finished studying for the day. I didn't think anything of it at the time – but I wasn't thinking, not with my brains anyhow."

"What happened?" Leticia's voice was suddenly hushed.

I lit a cigarette, and then went to the bar, dropped ice into a tumbler, and splashed whisky over the top. I held up the bottle in silent invitation. Leticia shook her head.

I sipped thoughtfully at my drink, and swirled the ice round until it clinked against the sides of the glass.

"When she unwrapped the towel, she still had her bikini on. Her nipples were hard. I remember that clearly. They were stiff little lumps against the shimmering fabric of her bathers and I gasped out loud and almost gave myself away. But she seemed not to have heard. She was humming to herself."

"And then...?"

"And then her hips began to undulate like she was in the midst of a slow erotic dance. Her breathing became harder and faster. She backed herself up against the bathroom wall and closed her eyes. Her head was thrown back, and she began to touch herself – gliding her fingers up and down her body. Then she slid one hand down inside her bikini bottoms and rubbed her pussy until she was moaning through an orgasm."

I finished my drink in a single gulp while Leticia sat staring blankly at a spot on the far wall, as if she were hypnotized. When she stirred again, there was a husk in her voice I hadn't recognized before.

"And then what happened?"

"She disappeared from sight for a long moment," I explained. "I heard the water in the shower running. When she stepped back into view, she untied her bikini top. She stood on tiptoes, with her hands cupped under her breasts and she pinched the nipples until they were hard little buttons. I was amazed at how large and firm her breasts really were. She stood admiring herself in the mirror – twisting and turning so she could see herself from every angle."

"And so you could see too."

I nodded. "Exactly. Then she disappeared from my sight again. I thought she was in the shower. I was just about to head back to the main house when something dark moved across the peep hole and I heard her voice."

"Oh, my God!"

I nodded again. Even now, I could remember exactly that moment of dire panic and horror – the moment I had been discovered. It came to me like a relived nightmare, detailed and textured. I remembered the hot flush of fear, and then a near-fainting sensation as all the blood drained away from my face.

"What did she say?" Leticia unfolded her legs and placed both her feet flat on the floor, leaning forward attentively with her elbows braced on her knees and her chin cupped between her hands.

"She was furious," I said. "She hissed at me. Her voice was low. She told me to go to the front door immediately, and if I wasn't there, she was going straight to my father. She threatened to tell him everything."

Leticia gasped. Her hand went to her mouth, brushed against her lip. "What did you do?" She leaned a little further forward on the chair, and I caught a glimpse of pale cleavage. The upper part of her chest was dusted with a light trace of freckles, and the creamy skin above the neckline of her sweater was tightly compressed. I looked away to refill my glass, and dropped in two more cubes of ice.

"I went to the front door – in a lather of fear and panic," I admitted. "I had never been so scared. This wasn't like facing an opponent in a fight – this was a totally new kind of fear. It was a guilty fear."

Leticia's eyes clung to mine, and then she started to shake her head with slow dawning realization. "But she didn't tell your father, did she? She didn't say anything. She'd trapped and caught you, and I'm guessing – from what you've told me already – that she started to blackmail you."

I smiled. I raised my glass in a mock salute. "Brilliant deduction," I said. "For that is exactly what she did. Claire blackmailed me for sex. She used me. Made me her slave, I guess. Over the weeks that followed she forced me to submit to her every whim...."

Leticia shifted in her seat, like she was trying to make herself more comfortable. She chewed the end of her pen and I watched her, saying nothing, but seeing the curiosity burning in her eyes.

"What.... what happened when you went to the front door of the guesthouse?" she asked politely, her voice very timid as though she suddenly feared I might deny her the rest of the story. "What did Claire say to you?"

I set my glass down and stepped away from the bar. I crossed the room and sat next to Leticia. Our thighs brushed, and I felt the warm suppleness of her flesh through the fabric of her skirt. She turned her body to face me. Her eyes were wide and luminous, and there was a sudden unnatural blush upon her cheeks.

"Before we go any further, I must warn you that the things I am going to share with you throughout this interview are very explicit. I can either censor the descriptions, or I can tell you in detail. The choice is yours. But if you want the detailed explanation, then you must be prepared for graphic language. I'm no fan of political correctness, so you can't expect me to keep apologizing if your delicate, sensitive ears are offended by language."

Leticia sat up stiffly; the sudden movement pressed her breasts hard against the fabric of her sweater so their shape became more clearly outlined. She clasped her hands in her lap and looked primly officious. "Mr. Noble, I am a fully trained and experienced freelance journalist. I deal in detail. Your language will not offend me, I assure you."

I sat back, and stared hard at her face for long seconds. She met my gaze, and her eyes were steady. "Fine," I said. I got to my feet and went to the window. The drapes were drawn. I edged them apart an inch and stared out at the night sky. Here in the hills, miles away from the city, the air somehow seemed clearer. It was most apparent at night. Overhead the stars shone bright and vivid, a million winking lights free of the filter of hazy city smog.

"When I went to the front door of the guesthouse Claire was there, waiting for me," I said, still looking out of the window. I dropped the curtains at last and turned back to face the room. It was gloomy. With only the glow from the fireplace, the light was soft, shadows darkening the corners and the ceiling. Leticia's face was pale and white.

"Was she angry?"

"She pretended to be," I said. "But when I saw her face framed in the doorway, I didn't see outrage. There was a flash of vindictive triumph in her eyes. She looked like a predator. It was in the glimmer of her gaze, and the way she held her body. There was steel in her expression, but I had the feeling I was a fly walking into a carefully woven spider's web. And I was.

"She accused me of spying on her. I denied it, of course. She slapped me across the face. She had pulled on a bathrobe, but the sash around her waist was tied loosely. It fell open and I stood there staring down at her breasts. She covered herself up and told me to follow her. I did. She led me into her bedroom and then she turned on me, shaking with sudden fury.

"She told me she was going straight to my father, and then to the police. That frightened the hell out of me. Maybe I could deal with my father's outrage if the whole incident could be kept private, but the thought of a family scandal –

the newspapers, the publicity – that truly terrified me."

"She slapped you?" Leticia husked.

I nodded. "She accused me of spying again, but when I denied it this time, I tried to tell her that I had noticed water leaking into the garden from the guesthouse and I was trying to locate the problem. She laughed. 'I know what you want!' she said. 'You want to look at my pussy. You've been crouched outside in the dirt, thinking about putting your cock inside me!'"

"What did you say?" Leticia whispered hoarsely.

I shrugged. "Nothing. I didn't get the chance. Suddenly Claire pulled the bathrobe off her shoulders and let it fall around her ankles. She stood before me, completely nude, and she was exquisite. Her skin was the color and texture of marble, her legs perfectly sculpted. She stood there with her hands on her hips and I couldn't help but stare at her. Then she reached up and grabbed a handful of my hair."

"Oh, my God," I heard Leticia whisper, but I didn't stop talking. I was in the flow of retelling the events, and the images were clear and vivid as though they happened only yesterday.

"She dropped onto her back on the bed and her thighs fell apart. Somehow I sensed instinctively what she wanted from me. I got down to my knees and she twisted her handful of my hair, but the rage was suddenly gone. Now she was consumed by something altogether different."

"Lust."

I nodded again. "It was in her voice. She was suddenly breathless. She was lying back on the bed and she was panting. She wriggled closer to me, and then lifted her hips. Then she pulled my head down between her thighs and I started to lick around her pussy until I discovered her clitoris and then ran my tongue up and down the wetness that was leaking from within her."

I heard Leticia make her own sudden breathless little noise. It sounded like a stifled gasp. I glanced at her, but her face was expressionless, though her eyes were suddenly wide and glistening.

"Claire threatened to tell my father everything if I didn't please her. She made me swear I would do anything she wanted – and then she came. Hard," I went on. "Her hips bucked and then she was writhing on the bed and moaning. She forced my mouth tight against her pussy. When she finally let go of my hair, I slumped back and stared up at her. She had her eyes closed and a dreamy smile on her lips. She was gently rubbing her nipples. I had the juice of her all across my chin. I went to wipe it off, but she sat up suddenly on the edge of the bed, her legs still splayed wide apart, and then she cupped my face in her hands and leaned forward. I thought she was going to kiss me," I shrugged. "She didn't. She licked her own juice off my chin and lips, and made satisfied little mewling sounds like a kitten."

I saw Leticia move on the seat, shifting her weight and re-crossing her legs. Then she reached down into her handbag and retrieved a new notebook.

"Do you want a light on?" I asked.

"No," she said quickly.

I hesitated. "Surely you can't see what you're writing in this gloom."

"I'm okay," she insisted. As she leaned forward, her hair rippled and swayed with the movement of her body. With the back of her hand she brushed it away from her eyes, then looked up at me, smiling. There was a sense of distance about her now – as if her attention was drifting, her focus wavering.

"Are you tired?" I asked. "We've been talking for quite a while."

Leticia glanced down at her wristwatch suddenly, and gasped with shock. "Oh, hell," she said. "Is that really the time?"

I nodded. "Maybe we should finish for today? We can always continue another time."

"No!" she said again, this time more urgently, and then softened her tone. "Not quite yet, please. I just need to hear the end of what happened. I… I hate having my notes and records fragmented and disorganized."

I didn't say anything. I shrugged. Time made no difference to me. I had no meetings for the next week.

I sighed. "Where were we?"

"Claire's bedroom," Leticia reminded me. "She had just orgasmed."

I nodded. "Yeah, and then she was licking my face. I didn't know what to do. I just let her. I thought that would be the end of it, but she made me stand up. 'Show me your cock,' she said. I got to my feet. I was hard. She stood by my side and kissed me."

I paused, remembering that moment. It was the first time I had kissed a real woman. I had kissed girls my own age before, but not a woman like Claire.

"Her tongue slid inside my mouth," I said. "And it was the most excruciatingly erotic fantasy I could have imagined. It shocked me. I felt it twisting and sliding. She sucked at my lips, teasing me and goading me so that when I felt her hand reach down and rub my cock through my jeans, I was close to erupting."

"And that surprised you?" Leticia mused softly.

I didn't look at her, I was lost in the past, reliving a watershed moment from my younger life. Finally I roused myself.

"It embarrassed me, actually," I admitted. "She slid one hand up beneath my t-shirt and raked her nails down my chest. It was like being clawed by a wild cat. I tried to flinch away, but she had unfastened my jeans and held my hardness in her other hand. Everything was happening at once. I had her tongue, sliding inside my mouth, and her fingers cutting into my chest. And then I had her hand wrapped around my cock, stroking me. My senses were reeling."

Leticia moved, stretched her back, then uncrossed and re-crossed her legs again. She leaned forward, staring at me intently, seeming to hang on every word, the notebook on her lap and the pen in her hand forgotten.

"She peeled my t-shirt off and licked the blood from the scratches," I explained. "Then she took me in her hands and stroked me. God, I was so hard. I was trembling. I felt my legs shaking, and all the while she was standing next to me, snarling at me and telling me how evil I was to spy on her and how I should be punished. She kept telling me she would tell my father everything if I didn't obey her. Then she told me to come. And I did. Everywhere. It splashed over the bed and then my knees turned to jelly and everything in the room started spinning."

I felt suddenly drained. The re-telling of that first time with Claire so long ago had left me weary. My throat was scratchy. I turned to the empty chair closest to the fireplace, sank down into it, and stared into the flames.

"It's late," I sighed. "That will do for tonight. I've told you everything about that first encounter, and I've been honest. We'll continue another night if you would like to hear more."

There was a long silence. When I turned around, Leticia was standing by the sofa with her handbag slung over her shoulder. "Tomorrow night? Are you free?"

I nodded. "Tomorrow night. At your place."

She hesitated and I saw the conflict play across her face and in her eyes.

"All right…" she said with slow caution, perhaps sensing that I was testing her. "I'll give you the address." She dug into her handbag again. I reached for her wrist to stop her. Her skin was warm and soft, her fingers long and delicate; the fingers of a piano player or an artist.

"I know where you live, Leticia. I've had one of my people find that information out long before you came here today."

Leticia froze, like maybe she couldn't make up her mind whether to be outraged or impressed with my attention to such detail. She looked up into my face with a silent speculation in her eyes. In the end, she merely nodded.

"Seven o'clock?"

She thought for just a second. "I have an interview with a tugboat skipper tomorrow. I won't be home until six at least. If you are expecting to be fed for your story, we will have to make it eight. I'm a slow cooker, and not a very good one."

"Let's make it seven," I said. "I'll take care of the catering arrangements."

She raised an eyebrow, and then smiled. "Seven it is." When she smiled, her whole face lit up. Her features smoothed out and she seemed to glow with health and vital energy. I liked her smile a lot.

I led her to the front door and in the foyer she turned quickly back to face me. She was blushing and she lowered her eyes and then lifted her face to mine.

"You were wondering about something earlier tonight, Mr. Noble. The answer is, 'Yes. Every day'."

She spun away, danced lightly down the steps, her handbag bobbing against her side. I watched her all the way to her car and then closed the front door quietly.

'Yes' and 'Every day'?

I frowned, stared off into space for a moment, and then suddenly smiled.

Lingerie!

* * *

"Will you be back late?" Trigg asked me.

"I don't know," I said. I lathered my jaw and glanced at myself in the bathroom mirror. The face reflected back at me was tanned, with dark hair that curled at the collar of my shirt. Hazel eyes and a mouth that was unaccustomed to smiling.

"Will you be contactable?"

I shook my head, tilted my face to one side and drew the razor down my cheek, leaving the skin smooth and brown. For a long moment the only sound in the room was the scrape of razor against stubble. Trigg glanced at me in the mirror and I caught her sulking expression in the reflection.

I said nothing more. Finally she left the room, taking crisp business-like steps, seeming to bristle with silent tension.

I smiled.

* * *

I turned my wrist to catch the light and checked my watch. It was 5:30 pm. The car was just pulling into the curb in front of the apartment complex. I leaned forward and gave my driver a tap on the shoulder.

"Good timing, Tiny," I said. He flashed a huge white smile at me in the rear-vision mirror. He was a big man with massively muscled arms. "Finalize the dinner arrangements for seven – exactly as I planned, okay?"

He nodded. "You got it, Mr. Noble."

The doorman outside the apartment building crossed the pavement to open my door.

"Good evening, Mr. Noble," the elderly man bobbed his head, his tone polite and respectful. "It's good to see you again."

"Hello, Hector. How have things been?"

"Quiet, sir," he smiled. "Just the way I like them."

Hector led the way into the lobby at a dignified pace, and a security guard was there to meet me. He was wearing a tan uniform shirt and black pants. He waited for me with legs braced, thumbs tucked in behind the thick leather band of his belt.

"Good afternoon, Mr. Noble."

I nodded. "Has she arrived home yet?"

"No sir."

"Very good."

We rode up in the elevator to the third floor and I followed the guard along a tastefully decorated passageway. There were framed prints on the walls, and discreet lighting built into the ceiling. The carpeting was thick: not luxurious, but not cheap either. The guard stopped outside apartment number 312 and unhooked a large brass ring from his belt, thick with clusters of jangling keys in every size and shape. He thumbed through the keys until he had the right one, opened the door for me, and then stepped aside.

I paused in the darkened apartment doorway for a moment, and then turned back to him. "You have my cell number?"

"Yes sir."

"Call me when she arrives downstairs."

"Yes sir."

* * *

Leticia Fall's apartment was gloomy. The last of the sun's rays had disappeared behind the distant hills, leaving the world in twilight.

I went into her living room and saw two straight-backed chairs nested around a small table. I carried one of the chairs through to the bedroom.

The drapes were open, the room filled with eerie half-light. Her bedroom smelled of incense and lavender. Just inside the door was a wide built-in closet, and across the room was a double bed with a small chest of drawers beside the headboard. I set the chair in front of the chest of drawers, facing the open bedroom door, and sat down.

I didn't think I would have long to wait.

My cell phone rang a few minutes later. It was the security guard's voice. He was whispering, as though he was part of some covert secret mission. I smiled. I should have given him a code name like Red Fox or White Eagle. I thanked him and hung up. Moments later I heard the front door of the apartment open, and then slam closed.

I heard Leticia come down the hallway in a flurry of muttered oaths and muffled sounds like a mini whirlwind. Something bumped against a wall – I think she was kicking off her shoes – and then she gasped. “Damn it!”

She burst into the bedroom and flung the sliding door of the closet wide open.

I sat silently.

Leticia hunted through the long rack of clothes. She swung her head from side to side, setting the blonde cascade of her hair swaying, and then tugged at the buttons of her blouse. She had her back to me. The soft silk slid down over her shoulders and I could see the lustrous skin of her back and the stark white straps of her bra.

She reached behind her and the sound of a zipper being drawn down was surprising loud in the silence. She squirmed and wiggled her hips like a dancer, and the skirt she had been wearing slid down around her ankles.

She stood on her tiptoes, staring into the dark recesses of her closet. I could see the firm toned planes of her narrow waist, the womanly swell of her hips, and the clench of her bottom. I could see the outline of her long sculpted legs and the tantalizing lace pattern of sheer white panties.

“Good evening,” I said.

Leticia yelped and spun round, wide eyed with shock and fear. Instinctively her hands flew to cover herself. She cringed in the half-light, hunting the shadows wildly until she saw the silhouette of me sitting by the window at last.

"Who the fuck –?"

"It's me," I said calmly. "It's Jonah Noble. There's no need to be alarmed."

"No need to –?" Fear transformed into outrage, her mood changing in an instant, bursting like a summer storm. "You broke into my apartment?" The tone of her voice was appalled.

I was sitting with my legs crossed, perfectly relaxed, with my hands resting casually on the armrests. I didn't move.

"No," I said. "The security guard let me in."

"What?" she was incredulous and disbelieving. "He let you in?"

"That's right."

"You... you... bribed the man?"

"No," I smiled lazily. "I own the building."

She shook her head and then scraped her fingers through her hair. She was trembling with the after-effects of her fright, and her breathing was ragged. She started to say something else, then realized she was standing half-naked in front of me, wearing nothing more than a lace bra and a skimpy sheer pair of panties.

She snatched at a robe hanging behind the bedroom door and wrapped herself in it.

"You aren't going to hurt me, are you?" Her voice dropped and became suddenly tentative. Her breathing was short and quick as if she had run up a flight of stairs.

I smiled wolfishly. "Not unless you would like me to."

She gasped. "What do you mean by that?"

"It's just a BDSM joke," I shrugged offhandedly. "That's all. You are perfectly safe, I assure you."

Leticia huffed and her expression became incredulous once more. "Relax? Are you for real? You broke into my apartment."

"I own the apartment," I corrected her. "This is just a routine inspection."

"Inspection? You son of a bitch. I'm standing here half naked!"

"Yes," I said admiringly. "But only half naked. I could have waited..."

I came up out of the chair slowly. Crossed the room. Leticia edged away like a timid forest animal. I held out my hands and kept my voice gentle and soothing.

"I'm sorry if I frightened you," I said. "But I wanted proof that you were being as truthful with me as I have been with you."

Leticia's breath quickened as I drew nearer. I stopped when we were only inches apart – so close I could almost hear her heart thumping within the cage of her chest and sense the ripples trembling throughout her body. The space between us seemed to tingle with electricity. It was dark outside now. Leticia's face was turned up to mine, her lips slightly parted, glistening soft and moist.

She swallowed hard. Her eyes searched mine.

"Proof?"

I nodded. "The lingerie." I reached down and touched the lace cup of her bra with the tip of my finger. "If you had undressed and were wearing cotton hipsters, I would know you had lied to me as you were leaving my house last night. You said you wore lingerie every day."

Leticia was backed up against the closet. I leaned an inch closer. I could smell the scent of her perfume and feel her nervousness.

She swallowed hard, and then her expression changed again. Her eyes lost their dazed, glazed mist and became clear and sharp once more.

"Thank God," she said. Her voice was a shaky husk, but only for a second. "I'm glad I didn't tell you I had pierced nipples and was waxed all over."

* * *

I left Leticia alone to change. She came from her bedroom ten minutes later wearing a t-shirt and faded denim jeans. I noticed she had touched up her make-up and brushed her hair. We sat across from each other at the small dining table. She flipped through her notebook to a blank page and set it down on the tabletop between us. Leticia looked up at me – the storm of outrage hadn't passed. I could see tendrils of anger in her narrowed eyes, like lingering smoke after a blaze.

"You had no right to break into my apartment," she said, and there was tight restraint in the way she spoke the words, like she wanted to say more, but was holding her temper in check.

"Like I said," I replied. "I own the building."

She shook her head. "That makes you a landlord, Mr. Noble, and tenants have rights. You can call it a routine inspection and you can brush it off, but I can't. You broke into my apartment," Leticia said again.

I pushed myself away from the table and started to rise. I didn't need this shit. I didn't need a lecture from a wet-behind the ears little girl. There were plenty of other journalists who would want the story – then I checked myself.

Okay, she has a point. You did break into her apartment, and you didn't have the right. Just apologize, and stop being an ass, Noble. There are more important things to worry about right now than your injured pride because the girl was offended.

I sighed. "I'm sorry," I said. I meant it. She must have sensed my sincerity. She did a thing with her mouth like she was trying to decide whether to accept my apology, and then she nodded slowly.

"Accepted," she said gravely, like we were negotiating a peace treaty across the table. The formalities over, Leticia seemed to let the tension go from her body at last, and shake off the dark clouds that had been building. She smiled suddenly, and it was a shy little gesture, almost like a peace offering.

"I haven't been able to stop thinking about last night, Mr. Noble," she said. "I've been distracted all day. The story you started to tell me has been playing over and over in my mind. I still can't quite believe how brazen Claire was."

"What I've told you so far is only the beginning of the story. I assure you, the best is yet to come."

Her eyes widened a little. She seemed to hesitate for a moment, like she was choosing her next words carefully.

"Mr. Noble –"

I smiled briefly. "Call me Jonah," I insisted. "Only my employees call me 'Mr. Noble'. Everyone else either calls me Jonah, or Sir."

Leticia nodded, then became curious. "I thought your submissive would call you Master? Last night you said –"

I cut her off again. "I don't have a submissive – at the moment."

"Oh. That's interesting." She scribbled in her notebook. "Why not?"

I shrugged. "Submissives are not slaves, Leticia. A slave is someone who obeys you in all things because they have no choice. In one way or another they are the property of the Master. They have no say. They have no rights. But a submissive is very different. A submissive can choose to leave the relationship at any time, and a submissive-Master relationship is very much one of constant sharing. It's like most other relationships, even though the dynamic might appear different to an outside observer."

"You mean someone like me?"

"I mean anyone who doesn't understand the lifestyle," I said.

"I'd like to know more…"

I smiled thinly and shook my head. "Not yet. *'Do ut des'*, Leticia."

She frowned.

"It's a Latin term," I explained. "It means *'I give that you may give'*. It's your turn to answer my questions about you. That was the agreement, yes? Our deal is based on the principle of reciprocity."

Leticia nodded with sudden caution. "Yes," she said.

I got up from the table and shrugged off my jacket. I hung it over the back of the chair and began to pace the small room.

"You spent your entire life in a small town, and then ten months ago, you suddenly left and moved here to the city. Why?"

Leticia sighed with weary resignation. "If you know that much about me, Mr. Noble, then you already know the answer to your question."

I shook my head. "I want to hear it from you. I want to hear the truth, Leticia. And call me Jonah, or call me sir, if you feel more comfortable. Stop calling me Mr. Noble. It makes me feel old, and I'm only ten years older than you."

Leticia sat forward in her chair, rested her arms on the tabletop. She stared down at her hands, and then looked up, her eyes filled with dark clouds and distant pain.

"I left my boyfriend," she said softly. "We had been high school sweethearts. I had been with him since I was sixteen. His name was Dwayne, and we were together for eight years, living and working in a small town. I was doing some waitressing work while I studied to become a journalist. Anyhow," she sighed, "One day, about a year ago, I suddenly had 'a moment'.

"A moment?"

She nodded. "I can't explain it exactly. It was just a moment where I suddenly looked at my life and saw it from the outside. I saw it for what it really was, not what I thought it was."

"And what was it? Really?"

"It was boring," Leticia said. "It was my mother's life being repeated. I could see the next forty or fifty years stretching out ahead of me with every day the same as the last. A small town girl who died a small town woman. The realization scared me. And it frightened the life into me."

"Meaning?"

Leticia was squeezing and clenching her fingers with anxiety. "I mean it made me take action. A week later I packed up and moved to the city. I applied for an internship with one of the local newspapers and got a twelve month trial."

I frowned. "Why didn't Dwayne come with you?"

Leticia made a brave face. "Because I left him," she said. "I ended the relationship."

"Just like that? After eight years of happiness?"

"After eight years," Leticia said. "But it wasn't all happiness."

"Did he cheat on you?"

She shook her head, like the suggestion was utterly ridiculous. "No," she said sadly. "It was even worse than that. He bored me."

"I see… In the bedroom?"

"In every way," Leticia said, then hurried on quickly, suddenly feeling the need to justify herself. "Dwayne was part of the problem. He was part of the whole small town syndrome. He didn't want another life. He had no expectations of anything better than what he was comfortable with. He had no ambition. No fire or desire to achieve anything. I was suffocating."

She looked up at me. Her eyes were luminous with unshed tears she was fighting hard to hold back.

"Do you feel guilty? About leaving Dwayne?"

"Sometimes," she said, then added quickly and firmly. "But I have no regrets. I did what was right for me. What I needed to do. Can you understand that?" Her face was pale and serious and her voice full of appeal.

I nodded, and stared hard at her. "Do you ever call Dwayne?"

She shook her head, and a single tear rolled down the soft skin of her cheek. "He's dead," she said softly, her voice choked with emotion. "He died in a car crash last winter. I went back for his funeral, and left town the very next day. I haven't been back again."

I stopped pacing. I was standing by the front door of the apartment. I turned away. It was difficult to watch her pain. When I turned back she had her arms wrapped around herself as if she were cold.

She stared down at the tabletop, but her eyes were vacant. The silence in the room was heavy, but like I said before, I'm comfortable with silence. I let it stretch out for long minutes until Leticia seemed to rouse herself. She cuffed at the teardrop suspended on her cheek and then dabbed at her eyes. She blinked up at me, long lashes glistening and dewy, and then took a deep shuddering breath.

"*Do ut des*," she said, mangling the pronunciation. "I want to know what happened next with Claire. You said your relationship lasted several weeks."

"That's right."

She caught me off guard, and won my grudging admiration. She was tough. The steely resolve of her nature that I had suspected lay just below the soft feminine exterior was there now in the way she dealt with the wounds and scars of her past and was able to move on – still function.

Touché Miss. Fall.

"I went back over my notes today," she said. "You also said *initially* your experiences were as a submissive. So did your relationship with this woman change – and if so, when and how exactly?"

I started to pace again and my mind peeled down through the memories until I was back on my father's estate during that summer with Claire. I remembered the smell of her perfume and the feel of her body. I remembered the sound of her voice, and the way her body writhed in the grips of orgasm – and I recalled those first intense weeks we shared; the madness and the dangerous passion of it.

I took a deep breath and loosened the knot of my tie.

"I went to the guesthouse every night," I said, "And during the days, when she was tutoring me, she became bolder and more reckless. It was like the thrill and the risk was intoxicating for her. I don't know if it felt almost like an incestuous taboo, because I was so much younger and so inexperienced, or if it was merely the excitement that all older women would feel in the same situation – but she quickly became more aggressive and more demanding," I said.

"In what way? Surely while you were studying your father would be nearby."

I nodded. "He often was," I said. "And we had a housekeeper and an elderly man named Oliver who tended the gardens. There was no place safe during the day, but that didn't stop her."

I paused. Leticia was bowed over her notebook. She glanced up at me, pen poised.

"She would brush against me like a cat, or lean so close over my shoulder that I could feel her breasts against my back. She stopped wearing a bra, and started wearing short skirts. I worked at an old desk my father once used, and studying was done in a room on the first floor. One day, after about a week, she came in and locked the door. Her face was flushed; she was trembling with some new excitement. She perched herself on the corner of the desk and stared down at me, her eyes glinting wickedly, her mouth almost twisted into a sneer. She rucked her skirt up around her thighs. She wasn't wearing panties. Her pussy was glistening with the wetness of her arousal, and as I watched, she slid one of her fingers deep within herself and let out a long low groan. She sucked the taste into her mouth, and then began to pant brokenly, like she was on the edge of coming.

"I got down before her and held her knees wide apart with my hands. She sprawled back across the desk and began to rock her hips. My tongue flicked across her clit, and then I sucked it gently between my lips. It was throbbing – pulsing. Claire began to moan, and the sound of her voice became so loud I started to panic that my father would hear us. I tried to back away, but she propped herself up on her elbows. 'Don't you dare!' she hissed at me, and there was venom in her eyes."

"What did you do?"

I shrugged. "I did what she wanted," I said simply. "I didn't have a choice. I licked her pussy, and a few moments later she came over my tongue."

"And no one heard?"

I shook my head. "But it set off alarm bells. I started to realize that it was just a matter of time." I smiled suddenly. "Don't get me wrong. I was in heaven. The things I learned with Claire were every young man's fantasy. She was sexy, she was passionate, and she was raw and intense. But she had a self-destructive reckless streak that terrified me. She was addicted to sex. As I told you last night, I couldn't afford to drag the family name through a scandal. I wanted the sex. I wanted it day and night. I couldn't get enough of Claire – even her perverse kinks – but I knew it couldn't be on her terms. I had to get control. I had to find a way to wrest back the power."

"And you did, right?"

"Eventually, but not immediately. I was still a virgin. For the first week or so I went to her bedroom every night and spent hour after hour pleasing her with my mouth. She would come in a writhing, groaning explosion, and then fifteen minutes later she would insist I do it again. At the end of each night, when she was so sated from orgasms that her arms and legs were like jelly, she would make me stand before her and she would stroke my cock. Sometimes she would lean close and lick her lips, as though she were just about to take me into her mouth – and then she would back away and laugh. Other times she was rough with her hands. When I was near the edge, she would cup her breasts together and present them to me like two soft milky pillows and I would throw my head back and come over her nipples. But that was all. The first time we had sex was when my father went away for a weekend business trip – and that was two weeks after she had caught me peeking at her through the spyhole."

"Tell me about that night," Leticia asked with a sudden flare of interest that startled me. "Did you know it was going to happen? Did she say anything to you that day? Why did it take so long, if she was so addicted to sex?"

I shook my head again, and looked up at the ceiling. "In hindsight, I realized that for Claire, the real thrill was the hunt. She was a predator. She was a cat playing with a mouse. She was teasing herself – not me. She was drawing out the moment, and torturing herself with the excruciating anticipation." I shrugged. It was the best explanation I could come up with.

"So you went to the guesthouse like every other night…?"

"Uhuh. I only realized something was different when Claire opened the door. She draped herself in the doorway, her hips tilted at an enchanting angle, and she was wearing nothing but a pair of lace panties. She was sweating. Her skin glistened and shimmered, and there was a sheen of damp perspiration between the cleft of her breasts. She took me by the hand and led me into the bedroom. It was dark. She had lit candles. I stood there in a state of wary confusion, and then she turned back to me and smiled. 'This is for you,' she said. Then she dropped to her knees before me and unfastened my jeans. I didn't know what to do. I stood there while she took me in her hands and stroked me. Her touch was gentle, and teasing. I closed my eyes, and felt the heat of her lips as she took me into her mouth."

"Was that the first time she did that for you?"

I nodded. "It was incredible. I felt this sense of giddy vertigo – a sensation I can't quite describe. I looked down and Claire was looking back up into my eyes. She had the length of me deep in her mouth, and her lips drew back and forwards as she bobbed her head. I reached down and tangled my fingers into her hair, and she groaned. That was it. That was all it took to send me over the edge. I erupted in her mouth, flooding come across her tongue. She swallowed hard, and she was smiling around my cock. I felt my legs trembling. I needed to sit down. I was sweating and shaking, but she kept me in her mouth and wrapped her hands around my thighs so I couldn't move. Then I felt her tongue slowly massage my shaft, and after a couple of minutes I was stiffening again.

"When I was hard, she let me slide from between her lips and she took me back in her hand, kneading me with her long delicate fingers. ‘Now you’re ready,’ she said. She was breathless. She led me to the bed and laid me out on my back like I was some kind of erotic sacrifice, and then she straddled my waist. Somehow, while she had been sucking me, she had peeled off her panties. I felt the brush of her body across my hips and she was naked.

“‘Lay still. I’ll do all the work’ she said. Her voice wasn’t cruel or insistent. It was a soft gentle whisper. She let her breasts swing forward and I suckled one nipple into my mouth. I heard her gasp, and she arched her back in a slow voluptuous movement so that her pussy grazed against the hardened tip of my cock. I felt the heat and dampness of her, and her gasp became a low moan of wanting that I had heard so often before. I think she had an orgasm right then; I felt little wavelets shudder through her, and she screwed her eyes tightly shut, frozen for long seconds.”

I paused for a moment and rolled up the sleeves of my shirt. I glanced at Leticia, but she seemed unaware of my scrutiny. She was staring off into the distance and I wondered what she was thinking, or visualizing.

“I think the idea of taking my virginity elated her. I think she saw it as a trophy of some sort. She reached down between our bodies and I felt the arm that was supporting her weight above me begin to tremble. Then I felt my cock slide deep inside her and she threw back her head and growled like it was a moment of triumph.”

I shook my head. "I didn't know what to do. My mind was reeling from the overload of sensations. Claire captured my wrists and pinned my hands above my head, then began to rock and undulate her hips, clenching and releasing her muscles, all the while groaning and gasping softly. She lowered her head and buried it against my neck. I felt her breath and then her mouth. She kissed and bit her way from my neck to my chest, and as she moved lower, the thrust and rock of her hips became faster, like a sensual gyrating dance.

"I felt myself racing to the edge, and every muscle in my body locked up. I forgot to breathe. Claire sensed it too, because she suddenly slid her tongue inside my mouth and kissed me so fiercely that she crushed my lip against my teeth and there was the taste of blood – and then I was lurching and heaving up off the bed as I came deep inside her." I said it all in one long rushed sentence and then took a deep breath.

It was warm in the apartment. The air was still heavy with the day's heat. I slid off my tie, rolled it into a bundle and stuffed it into my jacket pocket, then unfastened the top button of my shirt.

"Wow," Leticia said in a whispered, dream-like voice.

I smiled. "Every young man should have a Claire Moreland in their life," I said.

I meant it.

"Being taught the skills and thrills of sex by an older woman was one of the best things that could have happened to me, Leticia. I learned so much from her, and they were important lessons –

lessons I still remember and apply even today," I said sincerely.

Leticia looked surprised. "But she was crazy."

I shook my head. "Claire wasn't crazy. She was an intense, sexual woman. Sure, some of the things she did could be considered extreme, and I'm not suggesting every woman in her late twenties and thirties suddenly blackmail a teenager to be their personal sex slave. I'm simply saying that young guys would be far better at lovemaking and sex if they got their education from an older woman, rather than a porn website or one of their equally inept, inexperienced friends."

There was more I wanted to say, but the sudden sound of a text message on my phone derailed my thoughts. I fetched the phone from my jacket pocket and read quickly.

Leticia was watching me with an expression of vague concern.

"Anything wrong?" she asked.

"No," I smiled. "Everything is fine." I put the phone away and reached across the table for her hand. "We need to go," I said. "Dinner is being served."

She looked suddenly horrified. "I can't go out like this!" she looked aghast. "I'm wearing old jeans and a t-shirt. I thought when you offered to take care of the meal tonight that we would order Chinese, or pizza. Jonah – I'm sorry. I can't..."

I went round the table and pulled out her chair.

"Jonah, please," she pleaded. "I can't go out –"

I pressed my finger against her mouth, and her protest died on her lips. "We're not going out," I said calmly. "We're going up."

* * *

We rode the elevator to the top floor and when the doors glided quietly open, I took Leticia by the arm and guided her along the passageway towards a red door. Tiny, my driver, was standing in front of the opening, hands clasped in front of him, looking like a man-mountain – looking like a night-club bouncer. He was smiling. He turned and held the fire-door open for us and I led Leticia up the staircase onto the rooftop of the apartment building.

The night was still. A million stars hung in the dark sky, and a wedge of golden moon was rising from behind the distant hills.

The rooftop had been lit with hundreds of small tea-lights, their flickering flame spilling a soft glow as we stepped towards a candle-lit table set for two. A tall young woman was standing beside the table. She had long dark hair drawn back over her shoulder in a ponytail. She smiled politely at Leticia, and I pulled her chair out for her. She sat, in a bewildered daze, her eyes wide with wonder.

"I hope you like seafood," I said. "Due to the limitations of our location, I had to select the dishes in advance."

Leticia nodded numbly, and the waitress disappeared down the stairwell.

The city stretched out below us, the sounds of traffic rising and ebbing, the bustle of life somehow muted by our location and atmosphere. Pinpricks of light drifted across the dark landscape as cars and weary drivers made their way home from work, and the city streetlights ran away into the night like strings of sparkling diamonds.

"You did all this?" Leticia asked in disbelief.

I raised an eyebrow. "Don't give me too much credit," I confessed. "I just had the idea. Everyone else did the work behind the scenes to make it happen."

She tilted her head to the side, as if she were trying to see me from a different angle. She looked mystified, and she shook her head slowly. "You have a reputation for being a hard man," she said. "Everyone I spoke to told me you were a ruthless businessman. A heartless bastard," she said without any trace of guile.

There was a bottle of wine chilling in a silver ice bucket beside the table. I filled both our glasses.

"Guilty as charged," I said agreeably. "Whoever you spoke to is absolutely correct."

Leticia sipped at the wine and set her glass back down on the table, then leaned forward a little so I could see the candlelight reflected in her eyes. "Well I figured you would be a hard man away from your work too," she confessed. "I expected you would be just as demanding and just as ruthless in your personal life – with your submissives, I mean."

I frowned. "What makes you think I'm not?"

She looked surprised. "A candle-lit dinner on a rooftop? It's not what I expected of the formidable Jonah Noble."

"You're not one of my submissives," I pointed out. "And you're not a business rival."

She smiled. "So what does that make me?"

I considered the question carefully. I tasted the wine. It was good. "Right now it makes you a mystery," I said slowly. "A fascinating puzzle."

* * *

The meal arrived and we ate in amiable silence. The seafood was superb and I suddenly remembered how hungry I was. By the time dessert arrived, the bottle of wine was almost empty.

"What are the rules when it comes to BDSM?" Leticia asked. Then she frowned down at her plate for an instant before continuing. "I mean, *are* there any rules? Is there some kind of structure or framework to BDSM and the way people do it?"

I wanted to laugh – I really did, but the expression on her face told me she was genuine and sincere.

"Haven't you researched the subject? Isn't that what a good journalist is supposed to do?"

“I researched you, sir. You’re the subject of my interview.”

I nodded. “Well to understand me, you need to understand the BDSM lifestyle. Not many people do. Most people have preconceived notions about the role of the Master and the role of the sub. I think if more people understood the reality, they’d be less inclined to classify the lifestyle as abusive, or demeaning. Those kind of comments come from ignorance.”

She gave me a little smile. “So, enlighten me.”

I sat back and thought for a moment. I wanted to get up from the table and pace, but I didn’t.

“The BDSM lifestyle is like.... like seafood,” I said in a moment of dubious inspiration. “And seafood comes in a hundred different forms. Some people like shrimp, but cannot tolerate the taste of fish. Some folks enjoy lobster.... The point is, it all comes under the broad label of ‘seafood’, and yet we all have different preferences. BDSM is the same. As far as the sexual aspects of the lifestyle go, some submissives enjoy being spanked. Others enjoy being tied or handcuffed. Others I have met enjoy other things completely. It’s a question of taste, and those matters are negotiated by the Master and their submissive, to ensure both – I repeat both – people involved enjoy what takes place.”

I paused for a moment and studied Leticia’s expression. “Does that make sense?”

She nodded, though I could see it was conditional. She had more questions. I went on quickly.

"The only generally accepted rules of sex-play in a BDSM relationship are that whatever the participants engage in must be safe, sane, and it must be consensual."

Leticia waved her hands at me in a sudden animated outburst. "That's what I don't get!" she said. "That's the part about BDSM that I just can't get a grasp on."

"What? That it must be safe?"

"No! The concept that such a relationship can be consensual. How, for the love of god, is that possible?" Two glasses of wine had made Leticia animated. Her cheeks were flushed and her eyes sparkled. Her gestures, the tone of her voice, the way she held her body – everything about her became a little more real, and a little less restricted. It was as though she had begun to relax, and lost some of her prim reserve.

It had not escaped my attention that she had called me 'sir' just a few minutes earlier.

Had it been an accident, or was it deliberate?

"Leticia, if you desperately wanted children, would you marry a man that despised children?"

"No," she said. "That would probably be a deal-breaker, if I had my heart set on having a family."

I nodded. "Of course you wouldn't. And it's the same with BDSM play. No submissive is going to want to submit to a Master who is obsessed with whips and handcuffs, if they hate the idea of being whipped and bound."

"You're saying submissives have a choice."

"Of course!" I said. "More than that, generally speaking, in a BDSM relationship, the submissive is the one who holds the real power."

Leticia shook her head. "How can that be?"

"Because BDSM is based on consent," I said. "The Master cannot exert control and power over someone who does not willingly –" I raised my finger to emphasize the point, "willingly offer themselves. A Master without a submissive is a guy. Just a guy. He needs someone who wishes to submit to him, in order to become a Master."

Maybe I was doing a poor job of explaining the lifestyle, and the roles of the Master and the submissive. Leticia looked more confused now than when I had started with my ridiculous seafood analogy.

I really needed to get some better material.

The problem was that I'd never felt the need to explain the lifestyle to anyone before. Whenever I had engaged in conversations about BDSM, it was invariably with someone who already understood the lifestyle. I didn't have the 'sound bites' I needed to make a convincing case for someone like Leticia – someone who was outside the lifestyle, and with very limited sexual and relationship experience.

"You called the Master a guy," she said softly. "Can't women be the dominant one, and the man be the submissive?"

"Yes," I said. "Of course. Generally the stereotype is a male dominant, and a female submissive. But certainly the roles are equally valid if reversed."

For some reason I was getting annoyed. Maybe I was irritated with myself because I had failed to present the case for BDSM clearly. "But don't start that political correctness bullshit," I said. "I warned you last night. I'm not a fan. So if I call the Master 'him' and I refer to a submissive as 'her', you're just going to have to deal with it. Okay?"

Leticia flinched. I saw hurt or disappointment cloud across her face. "Okay," she said softly. She looked down at the table.

There was a long simmering silence.

I was the one who was simmering.

The shutters of Leticia's cool reserve were back up.

Noble, you're a jerk!

I checked my watch. The waitress was hovering discreetly in the background, waiting to clear away the table.

"I'm sorry," I sighed, and shook my head. "I didn't mean to snap. I got annoyed because I can't explain the BDSM lifestyle to you in twenty-five words or less. Leticia, it's not that simple – but no relationship, emotional or sexual, is easy to explain. It takes time to assimilate the information. I can tell you the facts and the way it works, but you can't understand them instantly. It's a process of awareness and understanding. That's why I knew an interview could never be completed in one session, and why you would never get a real understanding of the lifestyle if you asked questions that weren't insightful and probing – and very personal."

She looked up, smiled faintly.

I stared down at the dinner plates. "It's like – "

Suddenly Leticia leaned forward across the table and reached boldly for my hand. She looked up into my eyes and her expression was almost pained. “Please,” she said softly, with a mischievous glint in her eyes, “please don’t use another seafood analogy!”

For a split-second there was only brittle silence. Then I started to laugh.

And then we were both laughing and everything was all right again.

* * *

“Every night for the next three weeks I went to the guesthouse for sex,” I said.

We were back in the apartment. Leticia flicked on a lamp and then perched herself on a small two-seater sofa. I paced the floor between where she sat and the television. I glanced at her and saw her face lit by the gentle glow, and in that subtle light her features seemed to take on a new depth and dimension of beauty. I paused, distracted for just a second, and then continued speaking.

“Sometimes we would fuck, but most of the time she wanted me on my knees, licking her clit,” I said. “And if I didn’t do it right – if she didn’t come at least a couple of times – then she got angry.”

“Angry? How?”

“Threats,” I shrugged. “More threats to tell my father everything. Then one night she threatened to go to the press. That was it. That was when I knew I had to wrest the power from her. She was like a stick of dynamite. Sooner or later she was going to explode, and I knew the damage would be extensive. In short – I didn't trust her."

"What did you do?"

I smiled bleakly. "I waited," I said. "Then one weekend Claire said she was going to New York to visit family. Her sister had fallen down subway stairs. She left Friday afternoon, straight after study, and as soon as the cab disappeared out through the gates, I went to the guesthouse."

"You broke in?"

I shrugged. "I had my key..."

"You broke in."

I nodded. "And I went from room to room through the unit, looking for something – looking for anything I could use as leverage. I started in the bedroom. I went through every drawer and found nothing. There was nothing in the closets – I even went through the pockets of her coats and a couple of handbags she left behind. Nothing."

Leticia wasn't making notes. She followed me with her eyes as I paced.

"It was only a small guesthouse: no larger than your apartment," I said. "There was a bedroom, a small living room, a bathroom and a kitchen. Eventually, I found what I was looking for in the kitchen."

"What was it?" Leticia whispered.

"It was a diary," I said. "She had hidden it in the air exhaust vent of the range hood that hung above the cooking hotplates."

"God! She had a diary? She kept a record of everything you did together?"

"No. It wasn't that kind of diary. It was a small, personal one – the kind of thing women keep in their handbags."

Leticia sat back, and her shoulders seemed to slump as though she were disappointed.

"So there were no descriptions – no incriminating confessions like in the movies?"

I shook my head. "Sorry," I said, and then started to smile. "But there was a notation in the diary for that weekend. Just a brief little reminder...."

"Yes...? What did it say?"

I drew out the moment. Leticia was on the edge of the sofa. Somehow, during the course of our conversation she had become invested in the story, following its twists and turns.

"It was brief. Just a couple of scribbled lines. 'Meeting David. Excelsior Hotel. 3:00 pm.'"

"That was all?"

I nodded. "But that was enough."

"Who was David?"

"He was her husband."

"No!"

I nodded. "Yes," I said. "She had a husband. He was some kind of an engineer who worked away in the middle-east; a fifty year old guy with loads of money who worked overseas for three months at a time."

"My god!" Leticia breathed. There was genuine shock and incredulity in her voice. "But you told me she was divorced," she protested.

"She told my father she was divorced," I explained. "She lied."

"How did you find out this David guy was her husband? He could have been a friend."

"I phoned the Excelsior Hotel. I asked to be put through to the front desk, and then I asked if Mrs. Claire Moreland had arrived yet. The receptionist said she wasn't expected for a couple of hours, but her husband had arrived early. Would I like to be transferred to their room?"

Leticia gasped. She lifted her hand and pressed it to her mouth. "Oh, Jonah. Tell me you didn't…"

"I didn't," I said. "I hung up, and spent the rest of the weekend making plans. When Claire flew back in on Sunday evening, I was ready for her."

Leticia squirmed on the sofa. Her eyes were bright and shiny. She was looking up at me in anticipation.

"*Do ut des,*" I said softly.

"What?"

"It's your turn to answer a question."

"No. Jonah! Not now!" Leticia protested. "I want to hear what happened between you and Claire. I want to know how this affected you and changed your life."

"And I want to know about the most erotic sexual experience you have ever had."

Leticia sat back in the sofa with her face suddenly in shadow so I sensed her mood, without seeing it written across her face. I stood my ground and after a long moment she realized sulking in the dark wasn't going to change matters. She let out a long sigh and finally leaned forward, back into the lamplight.

She was suddenly embarrassed. "The only erotic experience I ever had was actually someone else's," she said softly.

"What do you mean?"

"I mean it never happened to me," she said. She made a little pleading gesture of frustration and then sighed again. "It happened to my girlfriend. I spent a Friday night staying at her home. Her parents were away for the weekend. We got high..."

"How old were you?"

"Eighteen," Leticia said. "Dwayne was working a double shift at the processing plant. My girlfriend and I got drunk on cheap wine and I fell asleep. When I woke up I was in the living room. It was late. I went upstairs towards her bedroom, but as I passed her parent's room, I noticed the door was slightly open. I paused, and heard my girlfriend's voice coming from beyond the door. She was panting. She was moaning and whimpering, and her voice was husky."

"So, what did you do?"

"I peeped," Leticia said guiltily. "I went to the door and looked inside." She hesitated for a moment. I stood, watching her patiently. She wasn't looking at me. She was gazing blankly into the darkness.

"It was my girlfriend. She was on her hands and knees, naked in the middle of the bed, and there was a man I didn't recognize behind her. He had his hands on her hips, digging his fingers into her skin, holding her in place as he thrust himself inside of her."

Leticia shifted her position on the sofa so that she had her knees tucked up beneath her. "There was a couple of candles burning – enough light for me to see the look of passion on her face. Her eyes were screwed tightly shut and she was groaning every time the man thrust against her. Her breasts swayed and swung beneath her in rhythm."

"Were you aroused?" I asked gently.

Leticia nodded. "The man was a lot older than my girlfriend. He might have been thirty. He had a broad chest and big muscled arms. He reached out with one of his hands and suddenly grabbed my girlfriend's hair. He pulled on it, like it was a rein. My girlfriend lifted her head and arched her back – and then opened her eyes."

"She saw you, watching them?"

Leticia nodded. "They both did," she said softly. "My girlfriend came over to the door, and she had a soft dreamy look on her face. She invited me to join them."

"And did you?" I asked.

"No," Leticia shook her head, with maybe a hint of regret in her expression. "Dwayne was my boyfriend. I wouldn't cheat on him. I told my girlfriend the same thing. She seemed to understand, but she could tell I was turned on. She would have been blind not to see it in my face, I suppose."

Leticia sighed and looked around the living room. She looked everywhere, except at me.

"She opened the door wider so I could see, and then she went back to the bed and laid on her back. The man got off the bed. I thought for a moment he was going to come and drag me into the room, but he didn't. He just smiled at me, and then stood at the edge of the bed and slid his… his penis into my girlfriend's open mouth."

"They wanted you to watch them?"

Leticia shrugged her shoulders. "I guess so," she said. "They started getting louder, saying all kinds of things to each other, like they were suddenly turned on by the idea of having an audience."

"Saying stuff?" I frowned. "You mean talking dirty to each other."

She nodded. "Uhuh."

"How did that make you feel?"

"It turned me on even more," Leticia confessed. "It was incredible. It was like nothing I had ever imagined before. Watching these two people having sex really turned me on, but once I heard them talk to each other the way they did – well I… I was…"

"You had an orgasm?"

Leticia nodded.

"Just from watching and listening to this couple having sex?"

She nodded again.

"What kind of things were they saying?"

"I can't remember," Leticia hedged. "But the words themselves didn't turn me on," she lifted her face and looked at me at last. "It was the attitude. It was the way the man spoke, the hoarse cry of his voice, and the expression on his face," Leticia explained. "And it was in the way he made my girlfriend pant and plead for more. She was wanton – a totally different character to the girl I thought I knew. It was as if the way the man treated her, changed her completely from a quiet nerd into a thousand dollar whore."

"Did he spank her?"

Leticia nodded. "A little. Not hard or anything. But he slapped and squeezed her breasts, and he pulled her hair. He called her his sexy slut... names like that. And every thing he did seemed to drive her wilder until she collapsed into a screaming spasm and had an orgasm."

"And then what did you do?" I prompted her. "Did you go back to your room, or did you talk to them about what happened?"

"Oh, god no!" Leticia cringed at the thought. "I stayed standing in the doorway. The man crawled onto his knees on the bed and began stroking himself. He was looking right at me. He seemed to be staring right into my soul. I watched him, and I stood there, while I felt his eyes all over me – undressing me – and then he suddenly cried out and groaned as he shot his stuff all over my girlfriend's face and breasts."

"And then...?"

"And then I fled down the hallway to my room. I was embarrassed. I didn't know what to do, so I went to my room. The next morning, when I went downstairs for breakfast, the man was gone. My girlfriend and I never spoke about it. Ever. It was just one of those things."

"Do you still think about that night?"

Leticia nodded. "Every day," she muttered wistfully.

She got up suddenly from the sofa, looking slightly shaky – almost as if she were appalled by the secret she had shared. "I need coffee," she said. "Would you like one?"

I nodded. Leticia disappeared into the kitchen and I went to the living room window. There was a view of the inner city. I stood watching the headlights on the street below, and I brooded.

My instinct was something I had always trusted in my business dealings, and with women. And right now my intuition was warning me: there was an opportunity here. It was a predatory sense – the same sense of the hunter who stalks a vulnerable prey. I sensed that within Leticia was a woman crying out for an opportunity to explore her sexual fantasies that had been stifled by a stale relationship and small town claustrophobia for too many years. It would take only a nudge...

There had been a time when I had seized moments like this with bold ruthless confidence. But now, as I stared down at the city, I sensed my own hesitation, and with it, an unfamiliar conflict.

'A fuck you knock back, is one you will never make up,' a business associate once told me, and I had pretty much lived by that questionable motto throughout my adult life, spurning every opportunity to develop deeper relationships with women for the freedom to bed whoever I pleased.

Leticia came back into the living room carrying two mugs. She handed one to me and stood there, shifting her weight from foot to foot self-consciously for a moment. I could see the turmoil behind her eyes. She looked down at the floor, then back up into my face.

"I can imagine what you think of me," Leticia began. "But I haven't had the exotic lifestyle you have lived." It sounded like a prepared speech she had rehearsed in the kitchen. "I've never been the kind of woman who would sleep around, but I would appreciate you not judging me as some frigid prude just because I don't have a long list of sexual liaisons, just as I am not judging you for your own lifestyle choices."

The speech delivered with suitable defiance, she took a quick tremulous breath, and brushed loose hair away from her eyes.

"I'll keep that in mind," I said.

We sipped our coffee in silence. Leticia fetched her notebook from the table and curled herself up in the corner of the sofa. She arched her eyebrows at me.

"*Do ut des.*" She got the pronunciation right this time. She was a quick learner.

I set the coffee mug down and my mind drifted back to that Sunday so many years before, when Claire had returned from the weekend in New York she had shared with her secret husband. I started to smile, remembering that night's events with fond satisfaction.

"I photocopied the page from Claire's diary and left it on her kitchen table for her to find," I said, picking up the thread of the story again. "Below her handwritten note, I had scribbled my own message, demanding she meet me in the study at nine o'clock. I was there fifteen minutes early. Claire was already waiting for me."

"Was she pissed?"

"She was furious," I grinned. "There was a wicked, malicious glint in her eye. I stepped into the room and she was pacing the floor like a caged lioness. She had her arms folded across her chest as if she was trying to restrain herself, and there were livid spots of color on her cheeks. She was literally shaking with rage.

"I asked her how her husband was. She glared at me, and told me I had no right to go into the guesthouse. I took the little diary from my pocket and taunted her by waving it in her face. I told her that little book gave me the right to do whatever I wanted. It was like showing a red rag to a bull. She flew at me."

"Attacked you?"

"Clawed at my face," I said. "She was desperate. She couldn't afford to lose her husband's money, and I'm sure I wasn't the only other man she had played her little games with. It was all falling down around her. Suddenly the boxing and martial arts lessons paid off. I caught her wrists and held them away from my eyes. We were pressed against each other. I could feel her heart racing like a trip-hammer. Her mouth was a red slash across her face. I tightened my grip – and suddenly something behind her eyes changed. I think that was the instant she realized I was a lot stronger than her. But it wasn't only that. There was suddenly something else in her eyes. It was arousal. She let out a broken little gasp and her voice was strangely husky.

"I pushed her back until she was up against a desk. Her mouth fell open in surprise. Then I spun her round and pressed my hand into the middle of her back. She folded forward, bent over the desk, and started to thrash and squirm. I ignored her. I held her down with one hand and kicked her legs apart. Then I reached up beneath her skirt and rubbed her pussy. She was wet – her panties were soaking. She groaned, and then suddenly went into another spasm of thrashing and snarling. I tugged the lace aside and slid two of my fingers deep inside her pussy. She arched her back and let out a sob of desire.

"I told her to lay still. She grunted. I slid my fingers in and out of her pussy and she started to rock her hips. I felt her push down hard against my hand. She was trying to grind her clit against my palm. I eased my fingers from inside her and reached round. 'Open your mouth!' I told her. She did. I forced both fingers between her lips and she sucked her juice from them."

I stopped talking. Leticia looked up at me. Her cheeks and neck were flushed with hectic color, and there was a trance-like look in her eyes. She looked away quickly and cleared her throat.

"How did it make you feel? Taking control like you did?"

"I loved it," I said. "It felt 'right'. It felt natural. I rubbed my cock against Claire's pussy and then thrust myself all the way into her in a single stroke. She groaned and I felt her hips rock and sway to accommodate me. I kept my hand pressing down between her shoulder blades and started to fuck her. She lifted her hips, and began to push back against me. I slapped her bottom so hard it left a red handprint on the flesh, and Claire seemed to suddenly thrill beneath me. It was like some deep shudder rocked through her entire body. I slapped her again, just as hard, and then drove myself into her until I was ready to explode.

"Claire wriggled one of her hands between her legs and began to play with her clit. I felt her fingers brush against my shaft as I was sliding inside her. I seized her arm and pinned it behind her back. She moaned in frustration. I told her she wasn't to come. She didn't have my permission. She started to plead."

I looked at Leticia. "That was the real power," I said softly. "That was what turned me on, and catapulted me into the world of BDSM. I loved the way Claire pleaded and begged for her release. It wasn't about physical domination for me. It still isn't. It's about that emotional transfer of power: the command and control. That's what turns me on, Leticia. That's what I find so addictive about being a Master. I love the power, given to me by the submissive. It's symbolic of their trust. Claire showed me how intoxicating that feeling could be. After that night in the study, my life changed."

I sighed. I was tired. I checked my watch. It was getting late. I massaged the back of my neck and felt myself deflate. I went to the dining table. I swept my jacket off the back of the chair and started to roll down the sleeves of my shirt. "I think we've covered enough for the night," I said.

Leticia came off the sofa, then saw my expression and nodded reluctantly. "Okay," she said. "I understand. When… when can I see you again?"

"We can continue tomorrow night, if you're free. How about my place, after dinner?"

"Sounds good," Leticia smiled brightly.

"Eight o'clock?"
"It's a date," she said.

* * *

I poured the glass half-full and swallowed it. Then I re-filled the tumbler and sank into the deep leather chair. This one I would sip slowly.

Leticia watched me with cool expressionless eyes. I slipped the knot of my tie and leaned back until I was staring at the ceiling. The old leather creaked and groaned around me.

"This is my office," I said. I took a sip from the glass and turned my head towards her. She was sitting across the desk, knees pressed together, hands folded in her lap, as though the setting intimidated her.

The walls were paneled with dark grained wood, the room lit by an oyster-shaped desk lamp and an old antique light fixture that hung from a chain in the ceiling. One wall was lined with shelves of leather-bound books, another wall hung with old artworks, their thick paint cracked with age, the frames heavy and ornate. There were intricate models of World War I fighter planes atop a long wooden shelf behind the desk, and on a lower shelf were dust-covered trophies and long-forgotten business awards.

It was a man's room. It smelled of cigar smoke and brandy fumes.

"It's... it's very severe," Leticia said politely, frowning as her eyes swept around the walls.

I nodded. "So was my father."

"Your father?"

I nodded again. "A lot of the things in this room were his. They're all I kept when I sold the old estate."

She glanced around the walls again and tried to find some kind of new appreciation for the room. She couldn't.

"Well... it's nice that you have memories of him..." Leticia offered weakly.

'They're not memories, they're reminders," I said and sat upright in the chair. "I filled my office with these things of his as a permanent reminder of what a bastard he was – and to ensure I didn't turn out to be the same kind of man."

"Oh," Leticia said. She was uncomfortable and lost for words for a moment.

And then she asked quietly, "Did you?"

"No... and yes," I said. "I'm not the same bastard my old man was – I'm a different kind of bastard. For him, power came from wealth and influence over businesses and his rivals. For me, the power I sought was on a far more personal level."

"Over women."

"Yes," I said. "Over women."

"So, why are we here tonight if this room reminds you of your father?" Leticia puzzled. "Why aren't we in your study, or in some other room of the house?"

I slapped the tabletop. "Because of this," I said. I rubbed my hand across the faded leather surface. "I wanted you to see it."

"The desk?"

"Yes. It's where the next part of my journey towards becoming a Master took place."

Leticia arched an eyebrow. "Should I make notes?"

"That's up to you," I said. I pushed myself out of the chair and got to my feet. I took another sip from the tumbler then set the glass on the desk. I needed to pace.

Leticia buried her hand into her bag for her notebook, then turned in her chair so she could follow me with her eyes. I prowled across the floor restlessly.

"After that night in the study, Claire knew I was in control, and although she still fought and defied me from time to time, she gave in more readily, until she simply stopped resisting and became obedient to my commands. In fact, I think she developed a taste for submission. Maybe it was something completely new to her – maybe she was discovering something about herself. Maybe it was an unexplored kink that turned her on," I shrugged my shoulders. "I don't know. I was nineteen years old. Some of the tasks I set Claire were things I am not proud of – but all I had to go on was the way she had treated me. At the time I didn't know any better. I didn't understand anything about BDSM. All I knew was that Claire had blackmailed me and used me for her own pleasure. I set about doing the exact same thing to her.

"Our encounters became a dangerous game. The thrill of having power over her body was intoxicating, but it wasn't enough. I started taking risks.

"One afternoon, as we were finishing study for the day, I summoned her to my father's office. I told her to meet me there at exactly 4:30 pm. I told her that if she was even a minute late, she would be punished.

"My father's office was on the first floor, a few doors down from the study. Claire had never been in the room before and the door was always closed. I knew my father was away until that evening. When I heard Claire knock, I was sitting in this chair, behind this desk, waiting for her.

"She came into the room cautiously. 'Over here,' I told her gruffly. 'Stand beside me and undress.' She obeyed me. She unbuttoned her blouse and handed it to me. Then she slid out of her skirt. I took it from her. She stood in front of me in her underwear, and I could see the anxiety and rising alarm in her eyes. She was scared, but the fear aroused her. She was sweating and trembling. I could smell the scent of her panic, but also her excitement. I got up from the chair and ran my hands over her. I unfastened her bra and her breasts fell free. I left the bra on the floor beside the desk and grazed my fingernails down her spine. She arched her back and purred like a cat.

"I sucked one of her nipples into my mouth. A rash of goose bumps spread down her arms, and she made a little choking sound in the back of her throat. I felt the nipple harden between my lips and I nibbled and sucked until she shuddered gently. Sucking Claire's breasts always aroused her. I felt her tangle her fingers in my hair to clutch me to her, and I slid my hand down and rubbed her mound through her panties. She shifted her feet wider apart to give me better access. My fingers slipped possessively inside the elastic waistband and I could feel the damp heat of her excitement. She shuddered – it was like a delicious thrill of anticipation. So I stopped. I grazed my fingers lightly across the flared swollen lips of her pussy and then backed away; left her on edge. I smiled at her cruelly. Then I ordered her onto her hands and knees and told her to crawl under the desk.

"When she was settled, I sank into the chair and looked down between my knees at her upturned face. 'Suck me,' I growled.

"Claire unzipped my jeans and stroked my cock. I was hard. I felt the warmth of her fingers as she began to massage the length of me and I reached down for a handful of her hair. Her mouth fell open instinctively, as I guided her lips over my cock.

"I glanced quickly up at the clock on the wall then closed my eyes. Claire took me deep into her mouth and started to slowly suck me. She made wet little slurping sounds. She licked and nibbled the swollen head of me and then engulfed my full length so that I felt her lips tight at the base of my shaft. She was holding me against the back of her throat. I held her head in place until I felt her begin to struggle and then reluctantly removed my hands. She came up for air, gasping. Her eyes were watering. Her lips were puffy and swollen. She licked along the hard length of me and then wrapped her lips back around the engorged head. I felt her tongue flick and slide, and the sensations were exquisite.

"Then there was a knock at the door."

Leticia looked up from her notebook in sudden alarm. "Are you serious?"

I smiled. "I am serious," I said. "I arranged it."

I stopped pacing and went back to the big desk. I leaned forward with my hands on the leather top.

"Claire gasped with panic. She started to squirm under the desk. I grabbed a fistful of her hair and twisted it savagely. 'Keep sucking my cock,' I snapped. She tried to pull her head away. 'Are you fucking crazy?' she raged, and I had to force myself back between her lips and hold her there. 'Suck my fucking cock!' I snarled. 'And don't dare stop – no matter what happens.'

"The knock on the door sounded again, and then old Oliver the gardener slowly pushed the door open and stood in the doorway.

"'Young Mr. Noble,' he said. He was surprised to see me in my father's office. He stood holding the door handle uncertainly.

"'Hello Oliver,' I said calmly. 'Is something wrong?' The old man shook his head, his expression puzzled. 'Not that I know of,' he said. 'But I got a message from your father to meet him here in this very office at exactly 4:45 pm. I don't know what it's about.'

"I made a show of frowning thoughtfully. Under the desk I could feel Claire's body trembling as she eased her mouth up and down my cock with agonizing slowness. 'That's strange,

Oliver,' I said. 'I got a similar message. He asked me to meet him here at the exact same time'.

"Old Oliver shuffled his feet for a moment. He looked down at the carpet and then back at me. He shrugged. 'Well, he must have got himself caught up in something. Can you tell him I was here and that I'll come back later?'

"I smiled. 'Of course,' I said. He started to pull the door closed. I sensed Claire suddenly relax, the tension seep from her body. I heard her stifle a sigh of relief as her mouth slid from my cock and she took me lightly in the palm of her hand.

"'Hey! Oliver,' I said suddenly. 'Why don't you sit here with me and wait for him. I'm sure my father won't be long. We could have a chat. I'd like to know how you're going with the roses'.

"I heard Claire gasp and then suddenly freeze. She made a soft choking sound of sheer panic and I thrust my hips up at her. Her grip around my cock suddenly tightened in panic. Oliver came into the room, and sat in the chair you are sitting in right now. He'd never been inside my father's office. His eyes swept around the room and stopped when he saw Claire's bra on the floor."

"Oh sweet god!" Leticia gulped. "You were insane to take that kind of risk."

I shrugged casually. "It was thrilling," I said. "That was what made it such a rush. The danger – the possibility that we might get caught."

"Did you?"

I shook my head. "No. Oliver said nothing. His eyes flicked up to mine and I could see the question in his eyes. I braced myself. I felt Claire shuddering like a frightened kitten, almost too scared to breathe. Oliver and I sat in silence for a couple of minutes, and the only sound in the room was the old clock. Finally he slapped his hands onto his knees and pushed himself wearily to his feet. He made a mumbled excuse about the lawns and backed out of the room.

"As soon as the door closed, I pushed Claire's lips all the way down to the base of my shaft and pumped her mouth full of my come. It was one of the most spectacular orgasms I had ever experienced. It left me utterly exhausted. My heart was pounding, and I was dripping with sweat. Claire crawled out from under the desk and she was so weak and shaken, she couldn't stand. Her lipstick was smudged across her face and her hair was a tangled mess. She stared down at me, her chest heaving like she had run a marathon. Her hands were shaking and her eyes were wide and reckless.

"For a moment Claire's expression was ferocious, and her green eyes flashed. I held her gaze and deliberately challenged her – dared her. She was seething. Every muscle in her body was tensed. I cocked one eyebrow at her in a cynical mocking gesture. Her temper flared for another instant, and then her eyes slowly clouded over and her shoulders slumped. She dressed and left the office without a word."

Leticia was watching me intently. Her expression was unfathomable. It could have been contempt. It might have been incredulity, or maybe something far more intriguing. Our eyes met, and then she glanced quickly away and took a deep breath. When she looked back at me again she met my gaze steadily, and I saw something move behind her eyes like a shadow.

"What happened next?" She asked in a whisper.

I stopped pacing. I took a deep breath then let out a heavy sigh of regret. "I never saw her again," I said. "Claire packed her bags and moved out that same night. I didn't realize what was happening until I saw the cab in the driveway and Claire standing there beside her suitcase. I watched her from the window. She saw me. Our eyes met for an instant – and then she turned her back, got in the cab, and it drove away into the night."

"You didn't try to stop her?"

"No."

"Did you want to?"

"No."

"And you never saw her again? Ever?"

I shook my head. "In hindsight, it was for the best. Claire sensed we were on some reckless collision course. We both knew it could only end in disaster. So she did what she needed to do to protect herself and her marriage. She did the right thing. The whole affair with Claire was a burning fuse. We were lucky it didn't explode in our faces."

Leticia sighed. She scribbled a note into her pad and then glanced at me with her head tilted at a curious angle.

"What stops a BDSM scene from getting out of hand?" she asked. "It seems to require a great deal of trust from the submissive."

"It does," I agreed, and then shook my head. The question deserved a more complete answer. "Write this down," I said. "I think it's important."

Leticia flipped over to a new blank page and furrowed her brow. She nodded, pen poised.

"Young men make terrible Masters," I said suddenly. "They're too focused on themselves. They get into the lifestyle because of what they think they will get out of it, not because of what they can share. Does that make sense?"

"No."

I took a deep breath and paced across the room. When I reached the door I stopped prowling and tried again.

"I've never met a man who I considered to be a good Master who wasn't at least thirty years old. Any guys younger than that only seem interested in their own sexual pleasure. They get involved in the lifestyle because they think it's a great way to get themselves off, without the burden of needing to feel any real responsibility towards their partner – their submissive. It's all about the guy's pleasure, and in those circumstances, the submissive is more likely to come away from a scene or a relationship feeling used and unsatisfied. Maybe even abused. I believe a true relationship between a Master and his submissive is as much about the emotional balance and interaction as it is about the sexual aspects. A submissive needs to have complete trust in her Master. She needs to know she can give her mind and body to him with absolute confidence that he will treat them as a gift, not a right. Women submissives are just as entitled to feel enriched from a BDSM relationship as their Master. It's a fusion of energies – a meeting of minds – and bodies. The woman needs to know that her Master will put her safety ahead of his demands, and her welfare ahead of his needs. Young men don't get that. They focus too much on the physical. They think BDSM is all about sex, so they make no effort to understand the submissive woman's mind, and how important her trust and her physical and emotional needs are to his pleasure."

I looked up hopefully. "Did that make sense?"

Leticia shook her head uncertainly. "I… I don't know. Um… can I read it back over?"

I smiled. "Do that," I said. "I need another drink."

I sank back into the old leather chair and splashed whisky into the bottom of my glass. From the corner of my eye I watched Leticia with covert pleasure until suddenly she looked up from her notebook and swept a loose tendril of hair from her face with her fingers. She tucked the errant lock behind her ear and nodded.

"I think it makes sense. It's a lot more 'normal' than I expected. I had the impression a BDSM lifestyle was all about extremes. You know… ropes and whips and leather…" her voice trailed off into silence.

"It can be," I agreed. "And for some people it is exactly as you imagine."

I sat forward and propped my elbows on the desktop. I studied her face carefully. "Leticia, there are no rules – apart from the safe, sane and consensual requirements I have already mentioned. If those conditions are met, then a BDSM relationship can be as extreme or as borderline-vanilla as the people involved want it to be."

She sat back and was thoughtful for a moment. She seemed suddenly reluctant.

"You can ask me anything," I prompted her gently.

She nodded. "I was just thinking back over what you said about BDSM relationships. It sounds all very nice, but it's exactly opposite to what took place between you and Claire. The way you treated her once you found out about her husband was the exact opposite of what you now advocate."

"You're right," I said honestly. "That's because I was a young arrogant fool, obsessed with my own pleasure and my thirst for revenge. I was the poster-boy for dangerous selfish stupidity."

"Oh," she said softly. "I... I didn't mean..."

"There is nothing to apologize for," I said bluntly. "Jonah Noble at age nineteen was a self-obsessed bastard. Jonah Noble at age twenty-five was still learning to understand women, and certainly not a worthy Master. It's only now – fifteen years after I first met Claire – that I consider myself a decent man."

"You're very hard on yourself," Leticia made a face.

"I'm no saint, and I'm not trying to become one," I confessed. "I've spent a lot of years learning about myself and learning about the women I have shared my life with. And it's only now – after a lot of mistakes – that I've finally worked out who I am."

There was a distant rumble of sound in the night and then a spray of rain against the window. A gust of wind rattled the glass in its casement. I got out of the chair and twitched the curtains aside. The night was black, seeming to match my own sullen mood.

I watched raindrops spatter and dribble down the windowpane and then turned suddenly. "I want to know your secret fantasy," I said. "I want you to tell me the sexy things you lay awake at night thinking about."

Leticia glanced up at me in dismayed alarm, and then lowered her eyes shyly. "I don't have a fantasy."

"You're lying," I said. "Every woman has a fantasy."

Leticia stared at me for fully ten seconds, and then a transformation slowly came over her. She got to her feet, set the notebook carefully down on the chair, and walked to the office door. She turned back, the space of the floor separating us, and she hugged her own shoulders as if suddenly she was cold.

"I... I used to wonder what it would be like to be blindfolded by a man," she said. She looked across to where I stood and her gaze was solemn and enigmatic.

"That's interesting," I said carefully. "Tell me more."

"What is there to tell?"

"I want to know exactly what happens in your fantasy, and how it makes you feel."

Leticia narrowed her eyes and chewed at her lip like she was making some kind of mental calculation. Then her eyelids fluttered and closed, and she stood with her back against the wall taking short shallow breaths as though preparing to face a firing squad.

"I'm standing in a candle-lit room," she said, and her voice was so soft the words barely carried to me. "It's a bedroom. I am wearing red lingerie. There are hundreds of candles on the floor and hung from wrought iron candelabras along the walls. The light has a golden magical glow, and as I'm staring into the flickering lights I feel my lover's warm breath on my neck, and then his strong hands on my shoulders. My skin tingles. I feel a delicious shudder run down the length of my spine. My breath hitches in my throat until at last I gasp.

"Does he say anything to you, this mystery lover?"

Leticia shook her head. Her eyes were still closed. She licked her lips. "He just reaches around and presses a silk blindfold over my eyes. He is gentle. He ties the knot tightly at the back of my head and then I sense he is no longer there – the heat of his body suddenly fades so that I feel like I am completely alone.

"I stand, not daring to move. My senses come alive. I can hear the soft sound of his footfalls and the faint scent of his cologne. And then I feel the brush of his fingers across the silk bottoms of my panties. I flinch. His touch is like electricity. I take a tiny step, and then I feel something ice-cold on my arm. I move again – just another small step, but as I do, I feel his soft wet lips on my neck and I start to tremble.

"Suddenly I realize I am lost – I don't know where the door is anymore. I reach out with my hands and my fingers press against his chest. His body feels like it is on fire. I feel the beat of his heart, and then he steps away, and the sense of longing in me is so strong that I groan aloud.

"An instant later I feel the teasing kiss of a feather on the tender flesh of my thigh. I feel myself clench, and then I turn and take one more step. Suddenly I feel the edge of the bed against the back of my knees and I begin to fall. He catches me, takes me in his arms, lays me down gently, and then covers my body with his own."

Leticia's eyes opened and she blinked at me. A self-conscious little smile passed across her face. She looked away shyly as a crimson blush of color rose from beneath the collar of her blouse.

"What happens next?" I asked.

Leticia didn't answer for long moments. She seemed still to be drifting amongst the lingering tendrils of her imagination. "Nothing," she said at last. "That's all there is. That's all there has ever been."

"You don't have sex with this dream lover?"

"No."

"He doesn't undress you?"

"No," she said again, more firmly this time.

I frowned. The rain outside became a downpour so that I had to raise my voice above the hissing sound as it overflowed the guttering and spilled down the drainpipes.

"Did you ever act out this fantasy with your boyfriend?"

She shook her head.

"Did you ever try to talk to him about it?"

"A couple of times."

"And...?"

"And nothing," Leticia said. "Dwayne dismissed the whole idea as a waste of time, and wondered why couldn't I be satisfied with what we were doing in the bedroom."

A wicked flash of lightning ripped the dark night apart. Flickering stark light filled the room for a split second, and the echoing thunder sounded like the roar of artillery. The rain seemed to intensify, and a swirling gale of wind flung leaves and dust and debris against the window. I stared out into the storm-filled sky.

"You're not going home tonight," I decided.

Leticia recoiled. "What?"

"You're staying here," I said. I turned to confront her. "You're not driving all the way back into the city in this storm. There are plenty of spare bedrooms. You can sleep here and go home in the morning."

She shot a speculative glance at me and started to protest. "I don't have anything to wear."

I waved her words away. "Then sleep in the nude. It's not safe to drive in this weather."

Leticia smiled at me graciously, and then lapsed into pensive silence.

* * *

The storm raged throughout the night. When Leticia came down from one of the empty upstairs bedrooms the next morning, driving horizontal rain still slammed against the windows, and the wind moaned and undulated through the swaying treetops.

Leticia looked tired. She had her handbag on her shoulder. She came into the kitchen the way a cat walks into an unfamiliar room – her steps uncertain, her eyes everywhere at once.

I was sitting at the breakfast table. Mrs. Hortez had extra places set on either side of me. She smiled at Leticia and shooed her to the chair beside me in a spatter of Spanish and nodding smiles. Leticia pushed at her hair and smoothed her hands down her skirt. She sat beside me and I could smell fresh perfume in the air.

"Sleep well?"

Leticia nodded. I slid coffee in front of her and she cupped her hands around the mug like it was the Holy Grail.

Over the rim of her mug I saw her eyes settle on the third place setting. She set her coffee down but said nothing.

There was bacon, eggs, toast, and more eggs. The aroma of cooking drifted through the house. Leticia seemed to slowly come awake and relax. She nibbled on a piece of toast and stared out through the big kitchen windows at the driving rain.

Footsteps echoed on the tiles in the hallway. Leticia turned towards the sound, and I watched her eyes carefully. Trigg came into the kitchen from the room I had set up for her at the back of the house. The two women saw each other at the same instant. Trigg's steps faltered for the briefest of seconds, and then she came to the table with a strained smile on her face.

"Leticia Fall, this is Trigg Alexander," I introduced the women and they nodded and smiled at each other.

"Trigg is an old friend," I explained. "She's staying here while her house in the city is being renovated."

Trigg was an attractive woman. She was a little older than me. She had a slim figure and long dark hair, pulled back over her shoulder in a ponytail. Her eyes were clear and grey, and her manner exuded an air of no-nonsense competence and efficiency. Trigg poured herself coffee.

"Nice to meet you, Miss. Fall. Did you stay the night?"

Leticia nodded, and I cut across the conversation.

"I wouldn't let her go home," I explained to Trigg. "Not in this weather."

There was a flash of something between the two women – some kind of intuitive assessment that was purely feminine and impossible for a man to understand. It lasted only an instant – a split-second electric charge that peaked and then began to taper without ever quite disappearing.

I turned my attention back to the bacon and eggs that Mrs. Hortez had piled up on my plate, and while I ate I imagined Trigg and Leticia standing beside each other – the younger girl's naïve, sweet innocence and gangling self-consciousness set against the poise and quiet confidence of a woman such as Trigg. Leticia would seem perhaps immature and girlish, and I wondered how much of Trigg's smooth, perfectly presented appearance would suddenly appear contrived without the natural fresh-faced beauty that glowed upon Leticia's skin.

There was a long silence. The only sounds were the sizzle of frying bacon and the gentle clink of knives and forks.

"I understand you're a journalist, Miss. Fall," Trigg spoke into the silence, and Leticia smiled graciously and then her tone became self-effacing. "I'm just an intern," she said. "I've got a twelve month trial with one of the newspapers in the city. Hopefully I'll be good enough to make a career of it."

More silence. There seemed to be nothing more either woman wanted to offer or volunteer in the way of conversation. I didn't spend too much time thinking about that. I waited until Leticia had finished her slice of toast.

"It's still too dangerous on the roads for you to go home."

She looked sideways at me. "Mr. Noble, I have to go home. I need to change. I..."

I shook my head. "I saw your car in the driveway. It's a little hatchback. A toy car like that would get blown off the road. You would end up in Kansas."

She smiled, despite herself, and I went on. "If you leave here today, it will be with my driver, Tiny. In my car. He can pick you up later tonight and bring you back if you want to continue interviewing me. By tonight the storm will have passed."

She thought about that like she had a choice. She didn't.

"Okay," Leticia nodded. "But before Tiny drives me home, I wanted to ask you a question that occurred to me last night, if I may."

"Sure," I shrugged. "I told you from the start – you can ask me anything about my life, or about my experiences in the BDSM lifestyle and I will answer you honestly."

Leticia looked thoughtfully down into her coffee cup and when she had her question framed, she glanced up at me. "Why doesn't the BDSM lifestyle work for more couples?" she asked. "From what I've read, and learned, it seems that lots of women want to experiment with the lifestyle, but their partners either are against the idea of trying anything new in the bedroom. Or – even worse – they give the concept a try and fail miserably.

"Now these are people in committed, long-term marriages, so you have to assume that the bond of trust already exists between them. Surely BDSM should work for these women, shouldn't it?"

I shook my head. "There are two problems. Men are scared of trying anything sexual they are unfamiliar with. And men have no idea how a woman feels. They don't understand what's required to make BDSM sex-play work for the woman."

Leticia made her eyes wide and raised an eyebrow at me in an artful challenge. "And you do understand women?"

"I understand what women need to make BDSM work in their bedroom," I said.

She sat back on the chair and reached for a new page in her notebook. "Well," she said with a smug little mocking smile, "this should be interesting. If you're right, then what you're about to tell me is the secret to success for the average married man. I'd hate to miss a single word."

I scraped my chair back and got to my feet. I started pacing across the kitchen like some kind of guard on sentry duty.

I stabbed one finger into the air. "Point one," I said, "is that men have a limited knowledge of sex. Generally their education has come from barroom conversations with their co-workers and buddies, and from reading things like '*Penthouse Letters*'. They never made the effort to learn about women. When they were younger, the couple of 'tricks' they used in the bedroom worked, and since then they've served up the same thing over and over again. It's all they know, and it's all based around their pleasure. That's not to say men don't make an effort to please their wives, but the fact is that most men are interested in pleasing themselves. The things they do work for them, and they always have – or so they believe. Anything new – anything as exotic as BDSM sex-play is so totally foreign to most of them, they are too scared to try it. Because they might fail.

"Men believe they can't possibly live up to their wife's expectations, even though most wives would be happy simply if their man made an effort. The guy thinks it is far better to avoid making a fool of himself by failing, than it is to try the things his wife wants – because he knows he will probably never fulfill her fantasies. No matter how low women set the bar – no matter how little they ask for from their man, he will rarely rise to the challenge because it means learning new things that he is uncomfortable with, and because it means he is going to stumble and fall along the way. His ego can't deal with that."

I waited for a moment. Leticia was scribbling furiously to get the last of my words down into her notebook. She looked up. "That's a broad generalization."

I inclined my head. "Sure," I admitted. "There are some men in the world who are experimenting with BDSM, because they understand how much it means to their wife. They are the exceptions to my rule. I take my hat off to those guys."

For a moment I lost my train of thought, and I couldn't remember why I was standing in the middle of the floor with a finger in the air. Leticia was looking at me expectantly.

"And your theory about women…?"

Ah. That was it.

"Women today are very different to the women of previous generations," I said. "The gender roles have altered. A woman now sees herself as an independent person, strong, opinionated – equal to a man."

"Right on, sister," Leticia said dryly. She made a little fist and punched the air. Then she shook her head in wonder. "The great Jonah Noble sounding like a feminist? Readers won't believe me."

I smiled. "It's a variation on *'know thy enemy'*," I explained. "If a man understands the way a woman thinks, then both people in the relationship will be satisfied."

Leticia stayed staring up at me for a moment longer, and then she hunched over her notepad and her hand began to race across the page.

"Because of a woman's newfound independence, the days of Neanderthals have long passed. Women don't want to be forced to their knees. They want to be made to feel weak at the knees. Husbands and lovers need to make the woman in their life feel *conquered*."

Leticia looked up from her book and shot me a short, sharp speculative glance. "Conquered?"

"Yes," I said. "Every woman who is aroused by submission is also aroused by an alpha male who can tame her. These women aren't looking for a husband in the bedroom who will make them feel safe and loved. They already have that in their relationship. These women are looking for a man who is strong enough to conquer them. That way the woman can still feel vibrant and independent... but also feel comfortable submitting to their lover. That's the turn-on for women. They don't want to be submissives... *they want to feel like they can't resist submitting*."

* * *

I watched Tiny guide the big car out through the gates and then I pushed the front door quietly closed.

Trigg was standing in the foyer, her arms crossed, leaning against the wall.

"She's falling for you," Trigg said softly.

I glanced sharply at her. "You're kidding."

Trigg shook her head. "A woman knows," she said mysteriously. "And she is suspicious of me. She is going to want to know more about us."

"You're an old friend who is having her house in the city remodeled. That's the story. That's how I want it. Leticia doesn't need to know anything more than that," my voice was cold so that it seemed my lips might be covered in frost.

Trigg made a small gesture of acquiescence and nodded her head. She stayed silent for another moment. "When she finds out – and she will find out, Jonah – she might hate you."

I sighed. "I know," I said softly. "But it won't matter, will it? It will be too late by then."

* * *

Leticia returned after dark. Tiny parked the car in the driveway and brought her in through the side door of the house. I was waiting for her.

She was dressed in a soft blue sweater and comfortable jeans. She had spent time on her hair and make-up. She glanced up at the night sky as she danced lightly up the steps, and then saw me and smiled.

I smiled back.

The storm had passed, but the weather had turned cold. The sky was heavy with dark rain clouds that hung close to the ground and blocked out any moonlight.

"Did you enjoy your day?"

She came in through the door and there was an awkward moment where I sensed her leaning towards me, as though to kiss my cheek. I flinched, and her head bobbed away, without the smile on her face ever altering. Her eyes were bright with energy and excitement. She stood very close to me and looked up into my eyes. She was trembling and bubbling.

"Fantastic!" she said. "I spent the whole day going over my notes so far, getting them in order."

I frowned a little, but her excitement was infectious. I felt myself grinning. "That doesn't sound like a lot of fun."

"That's not the fantastic part." She was standing so close to me that I had to resist the urge to slide my arms around her narrow waist and feel the warmth of her firm body pressing against my chest.

"The fantastic part was when I called my editor and the newspaper."

I took a small step back from her and slid my hands into my pockets. "I see."

"I read him some of the things you've told me, and he thinks it would be great copy for a four-page special feature in a Saturday edition."

"Wow," I said.

"Wow, indeed!" Leticia was brimming. "It's a big deal in the newspaper world, let me tell you.

The Saturday edition has the highest circulation for the week. It's the biggest paper the *Examiner* prints. And for an intern to be given so much space – " She seemed to get lost for words for a moment. She flapped her hands and drew crazy shapes into the air, "Well it's just the biggest thing ever!"

I smiled. "Congratulations," I said sincerely.

We went upstairs, past the closed door of my bedroom, and several other closed doors, to the library.

Leticia followed me into the room but stopped suddenly on the threshold.

"Wow..." she said again, this time her voice softer and filled with a subdued awe.

I didn't use the library any more. I hadn't been in the room for more than twelve months. The smell of old books and leather and cigar smoke seemed to linger in the air and permeate from the walls.

It was a big room. Every inch of wall space was given to antique dark wooden bookcases that reached all the way from the floor to the ceiling. There was a stepladder on a discreet sliding rail set in front of each bookcase, and the shelves were lined with an eclectic mixture of old leather-bound first editions, history books, mainstream adventure novels, and even some selected texts on occult magic.

There were thick Persian rugs spread over the top of polished wooden floorboards and two enormous wing-backed chairs, their soft green leather smooth and shiny in patches, as inviting as a pair of worn comfortable shoes.

The chairs were arranged across from each other in the middle of the floor with a small round table between them. On the table was a bottle of whisky and small glass tumblers.

I stood to the side, glanced around the room, remembering it all in an instant. Leticia stepped slowly forward like a sleep-walker. Her eyes were wide, her lips parted, her head tilted back to see the gold-leaf spines of the books on the highest shelves. Her handbag slid off her shoulder and fell gently to the floor, forgotten.

Leticia went to the nearest bookshelf and ran her fingers over the books, her touch like a caress.

There was an antique-looking chandelier hung from the ceiling, but it was actually a fake. There was a dimmer switch on the wall by the door. I turned the brightness of the lighting down until it was subtle and soft.

I sank into one of the chairs and poured myself a drink while Leticia walked along the shelves of books with a wonderland-like look in her eyes.

"I love books," I said. I sipped at the drink, sprawled comfortably in the big chair, and once again surveyed the heavy wooden cases. But for all the room's magic and mystery, my eyes kept returning covertly to Leticia.

"I like your outfit," I said quietly.

She looked at me and laughed in a low throaty chuckle. "Thank you for the compliment." She did a little pirouette. It was just a sweater and a pair of Levis, but somehow she made them look extraordinary. Her legs were long and slim, her bottom firm within the tight shape of the denim. Her breasts were accentuated by the way the powder-blue fabric clung to their shape and hugged at her narrow waist. She stuffed her hands into her pockets and turned back towards a collection of leather-bound first edition novels by a famous author.

"Do you know him?"

I nodded. "They're all signed."

She stood on tiptoes and reached up for one of the thick adventure novels, and the shift in her body only served to further emphasize the slenderness of her and the tantalizing silhouette of her breasts.

She eased one of the books from the shelf, holding it like it was some precious thing and flipped open the cover to the first page.

"For a man amongst men – my friend, Jonah Noble." She read the inscription aloud, then closed the cover and looked at me again. "Sounds like you have friends in high places. He's always on the best-sellers lists."

I shrugged. "He was close to my father," I said. "I kind of inherited that friendship after the old man passed away."

She carefully set the book back on the shelf and continued to wander while I watched her over the rim of my glass.

She stopped at the end of the bookcase and reached for a large leather-covered binder, thick with a layer of dust. It was on the bottom shelf. She knelt on the rug and opened the binder. I watched her expression.

Leticia's brow creased into a puzzled frown. She rifled through the pages, and then looked over her shoulder at me.

"What's this?" she was curious. "Why do you have copies of all these old newspapers?"

"They were mine," I said.

"You keep old newspapers you buy?"

"No. I owned the actual newspapers."

There was a long pause as the realization slowly dawned. She turned on me slowly, the folder still clutched in her hands. "You mean you *owned* these newspapers? You were the publisher?"

I nodded.

"You let me babble on like a school-girl downstairs, telling you about Saturday editions and four-page spreads when all along you were a publisher?"

"Yes," I said.

"Why?"

"Because you were so enthusiastic and so excited. It was the first time I had ever seen you like that."

She sat down in the chair opposite and slowly leafed through the folder. The pages were all yellowed with age, their edges tattered and curled. There were a dozen different mastheads from across the country.

"They were weekly community newspapers," I explained. "Years ago, my father bought them when they were about to fold, and we built them back up into profitable ventures."

Leticia glanced up at me sharply. "The *Examiner* is here."

"Yes. That was the first paper my father bought."

"But you don't still own it, do you? You don't publish the newspaper where I work – do you?" she suddenly sounded very wary, almost suspicious.

I shook my head. "No. We sold every one of those newspapers just before my father died."

I saw her visibly relax, and some of the tension went out of her shoulders.

"We ran those papers very profitably, but I could see the internet, looming on the horizon and building like a storm that was going to change publishing forever. I could see the writing on the wall for local community newspapers, so we sold them all at just the right time, and changed the direction of our investments into property – where they still are today."

"But you know the newspaper industry?"

I nodded. "I ought to. I personally ran several of those newspapers you have in your lap."

"Really?"

"Really," I said. "Once my father realized I was never going to become a lawyer, despite his best efforts, he decided the best thing I could do was learn the business I would one day inherit. At the time we had just acquired a new free weekly newspaper in the L.A. area. I spent twelve months running the business. In the process I learned about the print industry, and how to manage people."

Leticia sat forward. "What about women? Does the move to L.A. have anything to do with you becoming a BDSM Master?"

My mouth curled lazily into an insolent smile. "They overlapped," I said. "The office was staffed by eight women and one other man."

"How old were you?"

"I was twenty-four, and I was living thousands of miles away from my father's influence in an expensive apartment."

"I bet those women didn't know what they were in for," Leticia said. Her instincts told her it was time to reach for her notebook and pen.

I inclined my head, but I didn't smile. "Four of the women in the office were advertising sales reps. They were all attractive, well-presented – kind of like female real estate agents. Two of the other girls handled the accounts, and two were secretaries," I explained. "A couple of the women were happily married or engaged to guys with names like 'Skip' and 'Tyler'."

I refilled my glass and poured a little into another tumbler for Leticia. I didn't ask – I just poured, and left her glass sitting on the edge of the table between us. I got to my feet. By now, she knew what to expect. I saw her shift her weight in the chair, like she was preparing to watch a tennis match as I strode from one end of the library to the other.

"There was one woman there that caught my eye," I said. "Out of them all, there was one girl who had something special. She wasn't the prettiest, she was the sexiest."

Leticia arched an eyebrow. "Define sexy."

I shrugged. "I don't think I can," I confessed. "I don't have a definition, nor do I have specific parameters. It's not any one thing about a woman that makes her sexy in my eyes, it's a collection of things – an intoxicating fusion of the obvious and the subtle that merge together."

I replayed that explanation back over in my head. It sounded lame, but I had nothing better by way of a definition.

"This girl had 'it'," I went on. "She was one of the secretaries. Her name was Sherry. She was my age, but she was so dainty and petite, she looked like a teenager. She was barely five foot tall. She had this waif-like physique: tender pubescent-shaped breasts, delicate little hands. She had long black hair, and her skin was smooth and pale."

Leticia wrote it all down, and then sat back, gazing at me. Perhaps she was waiting for me to continue, or maybe she was imagining Sherry's slim body in my arms. I pulled my hands from my pockets and scraped them down my face.

"I was in a difficult position. My father had warned me about the dangers of *'dipping my pen in the company ink'*, and I still had memories of Claire that had stayed fresh in my mind."

"Claire?" Leticia was surprised. "Wasn't that years before? Surely there must have been plenty of other women between nineteen and twenty-four. You're a good-looking man. I can't imagine you had any trouble with the ladies."

"I did all right," I said vaguely. "And yes, there were lots and lots of brief encounters during those years. They were all learning experiences. I gradually began to understand a little more about what women wanted, and how they wanted to feel in the bedroom. But I mentioned Claire because of the blackmail issue. Now I was running a business on the other side of the country, but I was acutely aware that Sherry was an employee. I wanted her – fuck, how I wanted her – but I didn't want her because she worked for me and needed her job. Can you see the problem?"

"Uhuh," Leticia said. "But I don't see how you could have found a way around it."

I nodded. "I just couldn't see a way. Even if I invited her out for dinner, she would still feel like she was under some obligation."

"So…?"

"It turned out I had been agonizing over nothing," I shrugged. "One Friday afternoon as we were working in the office, Sherry propositioned me!"

"No!" Leticia gaped. "Are you for real?"

"Cross my heart," I promised, and she leaned forward in her chair conspiratorially as if she was about to hear some juicy new piece of scandalous gossip.

Her eyes were wide and hungry. "Tell me everything."

I chuckled. Being around this girl made me feel young again. "From the beginning?"

"And don't leave out a thing."

I closed my eyes for a moment and saw once again the narrow little office in east L.A. that had housed the newspaper. It was a run down little building wedged between larger, equally run-down buildings. The carpet through the office was threadbare, and the production area where the newspaper was composited was down a set of rickety internal stairs at the back of the building.

The production area was a converted underground garage; the floor was bare concrete, and the workbenches were arranged around the walls.

"Sherry worked on front desk reception for most of the day, and in the afternoon she would head downstairs to work on compositing the newspaper – doing the design and layout," I explained. "She would gather up all the editorial and pieces of ad copy that had been printed throughout the day and take them downstairs. Each weekend, we had a couple of retired old newspaper guys who came in on Saturday and Sunday and laid the paper out, ready for Monday printing.

"Sherry made sure everything was in place, on hand and ready for the compositors. It was part of her job, so I knew when she walked past my office with printouts in her hands, that she was going downstairs for the rest of the day.

"I waited about twenty minutes. It was early afternoon. I had a couple of messages to attend to that wouldn't wait. Two accounts had gone missing in the computer system, and the business was out of pocket a couple of thousand dollars unless we could find a tech guy to retrieve the information. Then I told Lizzy – the other secretary – that I wasn't taking any more calls. I headed down the stairs and found Sherry at one of the work benches. She was matching up long strips of editorial copy with a layout design.

She was leaning over the wooden bench, her legs slightly apart, her body tilted forward so that the short little black skirt she was wearing had ridden up across the back of her thighs and pulled tight across the firm globes of her butt.

Her head was bowed over the paperwork. When she heard my footsteps creaking down the stairs she swept the hair away from her face and turned. But she didn't smile. In fact she looked ill. Her face was flushed with color.

"I asked her if she was okay. She nodded, but then her eyes welled up with tears and I thought she would start to cry. She choked on a little sobbing sound, and then told me she had been the one responsible for the missing two accounts. She was shaking like a leaf. She looked up at me with big swimming eyes and her bottom lip was trembling.

"My first reaction was to get mad. I had spent half the morning trying to find those accounts and who had been responsible. I felt my temper simmering just below the surface. I stalked towards her and she bowed her head. Her shoulders began to shake.

"I stopped myself. I took a deep breath and clenched my jaw. And then, for some instinctive reason, I told her I should put her over my knee and spank her."

Leticia looked stunned. "How, in God's name, did you come up with a line like that?"

"I don't know!" I snatched my hands from my pockets and threw my arms wide in a gesture of wonder. "I don't know if it was some instinct I was beginning to develop, if it was some kind of sensory perception... to this day, I still don't understand what signals I had seen in Sherry before that moment that tore those words from my mouth."

"Did she faint? Did she run screaming?"

"No." I said. "She stopped breathing for an instant and the tears seemed to dry up in her eyes. She stared at me for the longest time and then she said, 'that sounds nice. I was actually wondering what it would feel like if you just kissed me.'"

"No!"

I nodded. It was true.

"She brushed at her eyes and then her hand fell away from her face and she put it behind her back. The movement thrust the buds of her little breasts against the fabric of her top. I could suddenly see the faint shadow of her nipples. Her breasts were so small, she never bothered with a bra. She lifted her chin in some kind of an invitation – or challenge – and then tilted her hip. Her gaze slid down my body and then came up again, and when she looked back up into my face her eyes were hooded and soft and dreamy."

"What did you do?" Leticia sounded slightly breathless. I heard a husky little scratch in her voice.

"I stood there," I admitted. "I was torn between acting on instinct, and my obligations to this girl as her employer. It was like struggling against a current of temptation and I was drowning. I wanted her. It boiled in my blood, blazed in my eyes – and then finally I crossed the small space that separated us and kissed her with a ferocity and angry intensity because I knew I could not resist.

"Sherry went soft and limp in my arms. The force of that kiss bowed her backwards so that she had to throw her arms around my neck and cling to me. Her mouth opened wide for me and I thrust my tongue between her lips and ran my hands hungrily up between the heat of our bodies until my fingers slid between the buttons of her blouse."

Leticia crossed her legs and wriggled in the chair. Her eyes searched my face intently, her lips slightly parted, her expression unfathomable.

"I slid my hand over Sherry's breasts and felt her nipples harden to my touch. She gasped into my mouth, and her body strained towards me. I broke the kiss and lowered my head to her neck. There was a sound in her throat like the purr of a cat and I felt her arms around me tighten and pull me down. I unfastened the first few buttons of her top and slid the fabric from her shoulder. Her skin was pale and flawless, her flesh unblemished and luscious down the tender line of her neck, and then firm and urgent in the almost immature shape of her breast. Her nipples were dark against the porcelain of her body, hard as pebbles, and a rash of tiny bumps rose around the aureole.

"I sucked her nipple between my lips and felt Sherry's fingers tangle and curl into my hair. I could hear the beat of her heart racing, and feel the pulse of her body change as I licked and teased the delicate pink bud until she was moaning and trembling softly.

"I wanted more. I was overcome with lust for this girl. I felt a red mist rising behind my eyes, and when I eased my mouth from her breast, my breathing was ragged. But it was mid-afternoon, and even though we were downstairs and away from everyone else in the office, there was a risk that one of the other girls would come looking for one of us at any moment.

"I slid a finger under her chin and lifted her face up to mine. 'What a precious, delicate little thing you are,' I breathed. She stared into my face with big wide unblinking eyes. I kissed her again and her lips were soft and wet and willing. Her tongue slid inside my mouth and she made soft whimpering noises. My hand went straight to her tiny little breast again and I pinched the nipple. She groaned and I felt her shudder like a tremor had run up the length of her spine. 'I'm not that delicate,' she murmured. Her eyes were dreamy, almost like she was drugged. I felt a growl in the back of my throat and I squeezed her nipple a little harder and rolled it between my fingers. She tensed – her body stiff and shaking – and then I stepped back quickly, out of arms reach.

"I felt like I was on fire. I felt like we could consume each other at that moment, and the heat would melt us both. My cock was straining in my pants. I stood back and looked at her, feasting on the slender shape of her body and the jutting swell of her breast. She made a move to cover herself – to pull her blouse back off her shoulder – but my hand snapped out and locked around her wrist. 'No,' I said. 'Not until I tell you to.'

"Something flashed in Sherry's eyes; it was like a flare of electricity. Her hand fell dutifully back to her side and she left herself displayed to me.

She lifted her chin, and her gaze was suddenly steady and understanding. 'Yes, sir,' she said so softly the words barely left her mouth, and yet they rang in my ears like some great tolling bell. I knew in that instant I had found the woman I was looking for.

"I told Sherry to cancel any plans she had for the evening and to meet me back at the office an hour after work. I told her to wear lingerie. She nodded mutely, and then I gave her my permission to cover herself. She buttoned her blouse and prodded at her hair. She was still shaking. I watched her dress, delighting in the way her delicate little fingers moved, and imagining them wrapped around the hard length of my shaft. I looked down at the smooth slim lines of her legs and followed them up to the hem of her skirt, fantasizing about how soft the flesh of her inner thigh would be to my touch, how tight her pussy would feel: how wet it would be, and how sweetly she would taste. Sherry stood obediently while I undressed her hungrily with my eyes. She was like a living, breathing sex doll – a perfect instrument for the giving of pleasure. The rest of that afternoon drifted by in a blurred haze."

"Did she come back?" Leticia asked.

I nodded. "I went for dinner at a local restaurant straight after work to fill in the time. When I got back to the office, Sherry was standing in the shadows under an awning by the front door, waiting for me. She was wearing a black coat and black shoes."

"What happened?"

I smiled. "It was the start of an amazing affair," I teased. "One of the most memorable times of my life – and I'll tell you all about the wicked ways of Sherry and the erotic BDSM games we played, just as soon as you answer one of *my* questions."

Leticia groaned. She slumped back in the deep embrace of the leather chair, like the air had been let out of her. She looked up at me with a silent plea in her eyes – which I ignored.

"When was the last time you had sex," I asked.

"Do I really have to answer that?"

"*Do ut des.*"

Leticia sighed, and then her expression became a little guilty. "About five months ago," she said quietly.

I thought about that for just a second. "So this was after Dwayne, right? This would have been after you had moved to the city to begin your internship."

Leticia nodded. "I was lonely," she shrugged. "I guess I missed home, maybe or missed the physical contact with a man."

"Was it a one time thing, or was it an affair?"

"Just one time."

"Tell me about it."

Leticia started to protest. I stared at her and my expression was like stone. She lapsed into a brief embarrassed silence. She lowered her eyes and fixed her gaze firmly on the notepad in her lap.

"I don't even remember his name," she shook her head shame-facedly. "I met him at a co-worker's birthday party. It was a big group at a local nightclub – maybe thirty or forty people from the office and all their friends. I didn't really know anyone apart from a few of the journalists. Everyone was drinking and dancing. I sat in the corner."

"Were you bored?"

She shook her head, and the blonde mane of her hair swished and glinted in the soft light of the room. "I was sad," Leticia admitted. "I was sad and lonely. I realized I was thousands of miles from home, and I was living alone. I had no real friends, no company. I had nothing but my work." She looked up into my eyes at last. "I made a poor choice," she said. "Not because I'm easy, Mr. Noble. I'm not that kind of girl. I made a decision because I was emotional."

I held her gaze. "Leticia, I'm not judging you."

She stared at me, said nothing. Her eyes went back down to her notes. "He was about my age. He was a friend of the birthday girl. He seemed like a decent enough boy. He wasn't drunk, and neither was I. After we left the nightclub, he offered to drive me home. I accepted."

"And when you got to your apartment?"

"I invited him in, and he ended up staying the night."

Leticia sighed. She wrung her hands like she was washing them with soap. "He was a terrible lover," she laughed suddenly, but the sound was bitter and hollow. "Can you believe it? After making one poor decision, I ended up choosing a guy who knew less about sex than I did. The night was a disaster. I ended up sleeping on the sofa and left the bed to him. I couldn't stand to lay near him – but it was me I was angry with. He was just a guy. I was the fool."

I stayed silent for a moment to see if Leticia would say more. She didn't. "What happened in the morning?"

She shook her head incredulously. "He told me he wanted to see me again. He told me I was a far better fuck than his girlfriend, and asked if maybe we could start something discreet."

Leticia looked up at me again and there was a dead, hollow shadow across her eyes. She leaned forward and suddenly snatched up the half-full tumbler of whisky I had poured for her. She swallowed a mouthful, and then her eyes went wide as if she had drunk poison. She tried not to choke as the alcohol fumes burned down the back of her throat and her eyes began to water.

She gasped and set the drink carefully back down on the edge of the table. I didn't bother to refill the glass.

"When was the last time you had an orgasm?"

Leticia flinched and her expression turned suddenly stony and cold. "I'm not going to answer that. It's *too* personal."

I sat back and slowly rubbed my chin. The silence crackled with sudden tension. She stared at me and her face was filled with defiance. I narrowed my eyes and came up out of the chair with slow menace. I prowled across the room, drawing out the silence, moving in the dull gloom like I was hunting prey.

"Leticia," my voice had turned to ice, "if you were one of my submissives, the first thing you would learn to do is pleasure yourself in front of me. It is a condition I insist every girl I train fulfills. Each time they come to me, they must undress and stand with their legs spread and their eyes fixed on mine. I make them reach their hands down inside their panties. I make them tease their clits and slide their fingers deep inside their pussies. I make them tell me how it feels to finger-fuck themselves before their Master – and they do it, Leticia.

"I let them get right to the edge of exploding and I tell them to wait." I said it all in a deep, low voice, my words rumbling. "And then I tell them to come. I order them to orgasm over their fingers and soak their panties with the hot melting juice of it. *So don't fucking tell me that asking when you had an orgasm last is too personal.*" The words flashed and sparked in the still air.

Leticia held my gaze for one more split second of defiance, and then she lowered her eyes. She cleared her throat and nodded.

"The last time I had an orgasm was just then," she said bashfully. "Listening to the way you spoke.... what you said... I... um...couldn't help myself."

* * *

I went to a bookcase set into the wall behind me and pulled out two books from one of the lower shelves. Concealed in the darkness was a *Romeo Y Julieta* handmade cigar, a cutter, and a lighter. I slid the books back into place and inhaled the earthy, aromatic scent that typified a classic Cuban.

I clipped the end off the cigar and inhaled until the tip was glowing and burning evenly.

"I led Sherry into my office. Now that the rest of the staff had gone home for the day and the building was empty, we didn't need to use the production room downstairs for privacy. The office was dark. I flicked on a desk lamp, but left every other light off.

"My desk was in the middle of the office floor because I had whiteboards along the back wall. When I had production meetings with the staff, I needed to draw up layout designs, so the desk wasn't at the end of the room or in a corner like most others. Sherry stood in front of me with her hands behind her back and I perched myself on the edge of the desk, swinging my leg lazily, the way a big African cat flicks its tail just moments before it is about to lunge.

"In the time since we had left the office, Sherry had been home to change and re-touch her make-up. I could smell her perfume. 'Take off the coat,' I said. Sherry slipped the belt from around her waist and let it drop to the floor. The coat fell open. I saw soft pale flesh and a pattern of intricate black lace. She shrugged the coat from her shoulders, making every movement slow and deliberate and tantalizing. Her eyes were fixed on mine, the heat and arousal in her gaze almost a physical thing. Her lips were slightly parted. She licked them and they glistened.

"The coat slid from her shoulders and fell softly around her ankles. She stood before me in just a black lace negligee. The dark shadow of her hardened nipples and the smooth cleft between her thighs was like some wondrous tantalizing promise. I came from the edge of the desk and stepped around her, inspecting and admiring her from every angle while she stood in silent obedience. Even in her high heels she barely reached my shoulders. Her head was bowed, and she was taking short sharp little breaths. In the silence, the sound of her ragged breathing seemed somehow magnified. I grazed the tip of one finger down the milky smooth skin of her neck and her flesh seemed to burn.

"I ordered Sherry to bend over the edge of my desk. She folded forward at the waist and instinctively separated her feet so that her legs were parted. I stood behind her and ran my hands from her knees up to the soft skin of her inner thighs. She shuddered. I could feel the heat radiating from her pussy. I lifted the negligee, like I was raising a curtain, and cupped one hand over her sex.

"Sherry sucked in a short ragged breath and flinched. I felt the flared, puffy lips of her, and the melting wetness of her arousal. My fingertips brushed the hard little nub of her clit and Sherry's hips bucked in reflex. I felt her sway, as though the strength had gone from one leg, and saw her hands reach out across the polished timber surface of the desk, her fingers clawing at the edge to hold herself steady.

"I asked Sherry if she knew what a safe word was. She shook her head. I explained the concept to her while the tip of my finger dipped in and out of her pussy. I told her the safe word would be 'falcon'. She had her head turned to the side, her face pressed against the tabletop, her mouth open and her eyes closed. Then she looked up at me slowly, like she was waking from an erotic dream, and she asked what she should do if she wanted *more* of what I was giving her, and never wanted me to stop.

"I told her she should beg."

Leticia stared away into the distance. "Sherry sounds like she was quite a woman. Did she have any experience at BDSM type sex before you two got together?"

I shook my head. "I don't know," I said. "I never asked her. In fact we never labeled the things we did as being BDSM. We simply fell into the sexual roles we were most comfortable with. I dominated her and she submitted to me. She gave me her trust and her body and her mind. Over the months that followed we learned about the lifestyle together. I guess you would call it 'on-the-job' training."

I smiled to myself. I liked that line.

I'd have to remember it.

"So what happened?" Leticia asked, dragging me back to that first night with Sherry in my office.

"I warmed my hand over the firm pale globe of Sherry's butt, and then swatted her. The sound of it in the big empty office was like the crack of a whip. It wasn't hard – I wasn't trying to cause any pain. Sherry flinched and let out a ragged breath, as the flesh of her bottom turned red. Quickly I smacked her on the other cheek, and she gasped again. I told her she sounded like she was enjoying it too much. I told her that from now on, her only focus was to be my pleasure. Then I ordered her onto her knees. She slid off the desk, and turned. Her hands went instinctively for the buckle of my belt. I smiled down at her, taking a savage pleasure in the way she looked up at me. She was eager to please. Her eyes were enormous. I let her unfasten my pants.

"I told her to open her mouth. She did. I told her to put her hands behind her back and to leave them there. Then I reached out and cupped one hand under her chin and the other at the back of her head. My cock was hard. I lined it up with the wet wide opening of Sherry's mouth and held her head still, as I guided myself between her lips in one long thrust.

"Sherry groaned. My cock went deep inside her mouth and I felt her tense and try to pull her head away. I held her there, and it took her a few seconds for her to become accustomed to the feel of me. When she relaxed, she looked up into my face as I began to use her mouth. Her eyes were watering. She was absolutely submissive to me – her body was mine to use as I pleased. I saw the silent joy in her expression and I gazed down at her fiercely, feeling my features begin to flush and coarsen with my own surging arousal.

"I eased my cock from her mouth and she gasped. She was panting. Her lips were swollen and puffy, her lipstick smudged around the edges of her mouth. She took two deep breaths before I seized her by the hair and lifted her to her feet.

"I spun her around and forced her up against the office wall. I told her to spread her hands and her feet. She pressed her face against the wall and stood there like she was being frisked by the cops. She looked back over her shoulder at me and arched her back so that her bottom was thrust out towards me, and she lifted herself up on tiptoes in silent invitation.

"I savored the sight of her. She was so slim, so perfect in every way. Her skin was pale, her waist tiny. I came up close behind her and I had my cock in my hand. I rubbed the swollen head of myself against the slick warm opening of her sex and Sherry's mouth fell open in a silent 'O'. She raised herself up a fraction of an inch and I guided myself into her, sliding deep inside in one long stroke.

"Sherry's body clenched. I could feel the grip of her and the pulse of her muscles as her body wrapped itself around the heat of me. She was wet and tight and warm, and I threw back my head and some kind of primal growl was torn from my lips. Sherry wriggled her hips and we became locked together like that, each of us lost for long moments. I clawed at her waist and buried my fingers deep into her flesh. I thrust myself deep inside her and then pulled back quickly. Sherry groaned. She braced herself against the wall and her hands bunched into tiny fists. I pressed one hand between her shoulder blades and Sherry folded forward at the waist. I seized a handful of her hair and pulled. Her back arched, her head was thrown back. I reached around her body and wrapped my hand around her throat. I saw Sherry's eyes grow wide and frenzied with sudden passion and she began to buck and push against me wildly. 'Can I come?' she gasped, her voice sounding like it was far away. I heard the sound vibrate beneath my fingers as it rasped in her throat. 'No,' I said cruelly. 'You do not come without my permission. I'm not finished with you yet.'

"Sherry whimpered. She bit her lip and closed her eyes. She pushed back against me with more determination and I thrust deeper into her with every stroke so that our bodies collided again and again as we built to our own climaxes.

"I dragged my hand from her throat and reached down for her breasts. She had slid down the wall and was bent almost in half. I still had hold of her hair, tugging it firmly as I drove my cock into her. My hand cupped the swell of her breast and I trapped her nipple between my fingers and kneaded it. Sherry grunted and gasped. Her face was contorted from the effort of withholding her release. 'I can't wait...' she cried out.

"I squeezed her nipple one last time and then thrust two of my fingers into her open mouth. She sucked on them, overcome with a desperate passion. I felt the slide of her tongue, and her head began to bob up and down, as it had when she was on her knees before me. That was when I reached the point of no return. I wrenched my fingers from her mouth and locked my hands around Sherry's waist. Then suddenly we were both crying out, our voices rising in the last few desperate seconds as I raced towards my release.

Sherry's cries mixed with mine. I heard her scream and squeal, and then I was coming, and so was she, our voices and bodies locked together in a ragged crescendo."

I stood silently, drawing on the cigar. My memories drifted back over those months I shared with Sherry, so that for long moments I forgot Leticia was in the room. I was a world away – another time and another place – and it wasn't until I heard Leticia's voice through the fog that I came back to the present with a start.

"Pardon?" She had said something I had missed.

"I said that you describe Sherry as a kind of nymphomaniac submissive wild woman," Leticia repeated. "Was she really like that?"

I looked stern. "Everything I have told you is the truth. Everything," I insisted, and then relaxed a little when I saw the flinch in Leticia's eyes. I drew on the cigar, and went pacing across the floor.

"Sherry had no limits," I explained mollifying the sound of my voice. "Normally a Master would speak to a new submissive about the activities they are comfortable being involved in. Most submissives have a set of hard and soft limits. Soft limits are the ones that are negotiable. They're important. Soft limits are those things that a submissive is reluctant to do, or might be unwilling to do until she gains more confidence in herself, or trust in her Master. The soft limits indicate the directions in which a Master can slowly begin to challenge a submissive – help her to broaden her experiences. Hard limits are those boundaries a submissive will not cross, and they have to be respected by a Master. Perhaps, in time, those boundaries and limitations might shift, or alter, but if they do, that decision should be the submissive's. In my opinion, a Master has no right to pressure one of his subs to alter her hard limits."

"But Sherry didn't have any limits, right?"

"Right," I said. "Sherry was willing to try absolutely anything and everything."

Leticia fell back into her chair and gave a soft little sigh. She glanced at her watch, and then started to comb her fingers through her hair. A soft blue cloud of cigar smoke twisted and hung in the air around the ceiling. "It's late," Leticia said, her expression almost tragic. "I have to go – but can I ask just one more question?"

I sighed. "If it's quick?"

She sat up, her expression suddenly earnest. "Who is Trigg? I mean, what is she to you, Jonah? Is she your submissive, or a lover…?"

I gave her a wintery smile. "She's a friend," I said. "That's all."

* * *

"Hello, Jonah? It's Leticia."

I had recognized her instantly, and I smiled. For some reason the sound of her voice made me feel absurdly pleased.

"Hello," I said.

There was the noise of murmured voices in the background, and Leticia's voice was a conspiratorial whisper, as though she had the telephone close to her mouth and her hand cupped around the receiver.

"I was calling to make a time when I could see you again. We didn't arrange anything before I left last night."

"Well I'm free whenever it suits you."

Her tone became brighter. "Great. I'm actually finishing work right now – I always do half-days on Friday."

I glanced at my watch. It was just after lunch. "Do you want to come over this afternoon?"

Leticia hesitated. "Well, I was actually wondering if you would like to come to my place tonight – for dinner. I told you I was a slow cooker. I figured with an entire afternoon to prepare, I should be able to feed you something that wouldn't be burned."

I smiled into the phone. "Sure," I said. "That sounds fine. What time do you want me there?"

"Six? Is that too early?"

"Six will be fine."

"Wonderful," she seemed relieved. "I'll see you then."

She sounded like she was about to end the call and I cut in quickly. "Do you want me to bring anything – fire extinguisher, or maybe a bottle of wine?"

"I'm not that bad a cook, mister!" she feigned umbrage. "But some wine would be nice. I'm in the mood for a drink."

* * *

I always arrive five minutes early.

I'm never late.

Ever.

It's a habit I developed at an early age, and one I adhere to ruthlessly. I believe it's a sign of courtesy, but also a measure of how much importance you place on the meeting, and whom it is you are about to meet. Arriving ten minutes late anywhere is a sign of arrogance, in Jonah Noble's big book of rules to live by. Turning up anywhere late says – loud and clear – that you're more important than the person who is expecting you, so they can damned-well wait until you're good and ready to grace them with your presence.

I had been known to dismiss submissives for arriving to training sessions late, sending them home in devastated tears. And I have been known to break off business deals, simply because the other guy was unable to get his ass to a meeting on time.

So when Tiny parked the car in front of Leticia's apartment block, it was several minutes before six o'clock. Old Hector, the doorman, came from the shadows under the awning and shuffled across the pavement.

I got out of the car and leaned back in through the window. "Take yourself out for dinner, Tiny," I reached into my wallet and pressed money into his huge hand. "You look like you could do with a decent feed. I'll call you when I'm ready to leave."

The giant man's face split into a surprised smile. He threw me a playful salute, and the car pulled away into the evening traffic. Hector walked with me into the foyer and we spent a couple of minutes chatting.

I rode the elevator to Leticia's floor, and knocked on the door. I heard her squeal in panic, and then the sound of footsteps.

"You can't come in!" she shouted through the door. "I need three more minutes, okay?"

"Sure," I smiled.

I went pacing back down the passageway. I tucked the bottle of wine under my arm and checked my phone. There was a message from Trigg. I didn't read it.

Then I saw the door to Leticia's apartment flung open and her head popped out through the doorway. She looked left, then right – saw me at last, and her face brightened into a wide happy grin.

Leticia held the door open and stood back anxiously. I stepped over the threshold.

The apartment was filled with the aromas of roast meat and vegetables; the kind of country home-cooking that makes a man's mouth water. I saw a splash of fresh flowers in a vase on the table, and I got the sense that the whole apartment had been cleaned. I set the wine down beside the flower arrangement and then raised my eyebrows as I turned to Leticia.

She was wearing a simple white cotton dress. It bulged around the firm press of her breasts, clung to the form of her waist, and ended just above her knees. She wore makeup, and I noticed a delicate silver bracelet around her wrist.

"What do you think?" Leticia waved her arms wide.

"I think you look... beautiful," I said into the expectant silence. Leticia seemed to melt just a little, and then she blushed and transformed from a young woman into a shy sixteen-year-old girl for an instant, then back again. She looked up into my face with a yearning little expression, like a flower leaning towards the sunshine. "Thank you," she whispered. She stood disconcertingly close, enveloping me with her scent. I could see the agitated rise and fall of her breasts under the thin cotton. She seemed to catch her breath for an instant. Her lips were soft and glossy…

I glanced towards the kitchen to distract myself. "Dinner smells great," I said abruptly. I turned on my heel, thrust my tense fists deep into my pockets and cast my eyes around the walls, giving myself time and breaking the spell of dangerous intimacy.

Leticia's smile was brittle: too wide and bright to be natural. She flitted around the apartment fluffing sofa pillows and straightening magazines. "I hope you like roast lamb."

She went into the kitchen, and I opened the bottle of wine. When Leticia came back into the living room, she was carrying plates.

The food was sensational. Despite her self-depreciating comments, Leticia was actually a wonderful cook. I poured wine for us both and we laughed and talked easily until the meal was finished and the plates cleared away.

Leticia led me towards the sofa. She drew her legs up beneath her and I saw a flash of toned brown thigh before she arranged the fabric of her dress around her and reached for the notebook.

"Last night you told me about your first time with Sherry," she reminded me. "You said it was the start of a sexy affair that lasted for several months. I'd like to know more..."

I stared down into my wine glass. "Unlike Claire Moreland, Sherry was very discreet – very composed," I said. "No one in the office had the slightest idea anything was going on between the two of us. Sherry did her job and kept her routines. I was painfully aware that everything should appear normal to the rest of the staff, so I was careful in what we did – but we still did plenty of things as the days between our Friday night sex sessions seemed to drag on forever."

"What kind of things?" Leticia was curious. "Surely if your contact was limited...?"

"It was, but there were still opportunities. "Sometimes I would call her into my office to collect layout pages for the next edition. She would stand at the side of my desk and I would explain how I wanted the pages set up. While she was leaning over my desk I would slide my hand up her skirt. She was always wet, and she would stand there and make banal little comments like 'yes, I see...' or 'what about the photos for that story...' while I was sliding two fingers inside her pussy and she was biting her lip and trying not to groan aloud."

I could no longer remain seated. I stood up and began to pace the floor, looking down at the glass of wine in my hand.

"I ordered her to stop wearing panties to work, and each morning she would come into my office to hand me the overnight messages that had been left on the answering machine. It was inspection time and she would dutifully pull the hem of her skirt high so that I could see she was indeed following my orders. Sometimes, while she stood there, I would tell her to finger herself – but it always had to be quick. Sherry was in a permanent state of arousal. She shaved her pussy completely smooth so I could see her delicate little fingers rub her clit until they became sticky with her juices, and I would tell her to rub the essence on her lips and wear it like lip gloss. She did everything I ordered her to."

"And what about you?" Leticia asked. "Was it arousing for you?"

"Sure," I nodded. "It turned me on to see her following my instructions without question, and to watch her masturbate. Sometimes, if she arrived at work before the other girls, I had time to slide my cock into her mouth, but usually the tasks were all about keeping Sherry aroused, and subtly creating a system of command and obey, where she learned to submit herself to a series of small challenges.

"As I explained, most of the tasks were actually forms of training: wearing no panties during the day, fingering herself while I watched, and even keeping her pussy shaved so that it was always soft and smooth for my pleasure were actually training techniques that I still use with submissives to this day."

Leticia looked up at me with growing interest. She set her notebook down for a moment and her eyes became hooded.

"Do you like all your women shaved down there, Jonah?" she asked softly.

"I insist on it," I said. "It pleases me."

I retrieved the wine bottle and shared the last of its contents between our two glasses. I left Leticia's drink on the coffee table and went across to the window. Leticia was watching me, her expression unfathomable, and I wondered what dark mysterious thoughts were going on behind her eyes.

"The fact that Sherry needed to be in my office often was a bonus," I went on. "But she couldn't stay for more than a few minutes – that would raise suspicion. But she was always seeking clarifications on the layout of the paper, so our contact was regular, yet always fleeting. One morning I gave her a thick whiteboard marker pen. I used several of them for drawing up the next edition of the newspaper. I placed the pen in her hand and told her to take it to the washroom and use it to make herself come. Sherry looked down at the marker and merely nodded obediently. I went back to work, but it was hard to concentrate. I imagined her with her legs wide apart, her skirt up around her waist and the thick pen sliding slowly in and out of herself. In my imagination I saw the way her pussy lips would flare and wrap tight around the shaft, and how hard it would feel inside her. I thought about her rubbing her clit, and visualized the look on her face as she brought herself off. It was incredibly arousing."

"She used it like a… a sex toy?"

I nodded. "Sherry came back into my office about ten minutes later. She was all very calm, as if nothing had happened. She simply handed the marker pen back to me casually and said, 'oh, here is the pen back that I borrowed, Mr. Noble'. When I looked down, the marker was coated in a slick layer of her sex juices."

Leticia scribbled into her notebook, and then set her pen down. I was leaning against the windowsill with one hand in my pocket and my legs stretched out, ankles crossed. I finished the last of the wine.

"Why do you think the BDSM lifestyle has become so popular all of a sudden?" Leticia asked. "Everywhere I go there seems to be information and articles and images that weren't there before."

I shrugged my shoulders. "Well unless you hadn't heard, there was a particular novel that was very popular with ladies," I smiled briefly, and then gave the question more serious thought. I pushed myself away from the window and stood in the middle of the floor. "That book certainly created tremendous awareness, but more than that, I think it sparked women's imaginations and made them look more closely at their lives."

"Meaning?"

"Meaning that I think women want men to be more like men again," I said. "The world went through a bizarre stage for a while where men changed. They started using 'product' in their hair and wearing make up for Christ's sake! Men, wearing concealer and foundation and hair gel and eyeliner... doing everything they could to look like women. I think women got fed up with all that. I think women suddenly realized that in order for them to be made to feel like a woman, they needed men to act like real men again.

"A real man stands in the bathroom doorway watching his woman putting on her makeup, and he's overcome with desire. His eyes roam up and down the woman's figure, and suddenly there is a spark of lust in his eyes. The woman sees it in the reflection. She knows that look, and she feels a tiny tremor of anticipation. The man steps up behind the woman and there is a growl in the back of his throat as he slides his hands up across her hips and around her waist. He pulls the woman back against him and she can feel the hardness of his erection. The man's hands are suddenly all over her – caressing her breasts and sliding down the flat of her abdomen towards her panties. He bites her neck and the woman's breathing quickens. She has turned him on, and now the man wants her – and she needs to feel wanted. That's the way it should be."

I shook my head. I heard the echo of my own voice and realized I was speaking with genuine passion. "The man doesn't see his woman in the bathroom mirror putting on makeup and ask if he can borrow some eye shadow!"

I took a deep breath. Maybe my rant had taken me off topic. I sighed. "Leticia, BDSM has always been part of our society. Maybe it has never grabbed the headlines before, but it has always been there, and it always will. The fact that more women are aware of the lifestyle choice now is a good thing. Choice means options, and there are a lot of ladies in stifled marriages that know there must be more to living than the boring routine they have suffered through for years. They look to their husband as the first choice to satisfy that new awareness – that new yearning for more. And that means husbands across the country have to up their game. They have to re-discover their manly instinct and drag their butts out of the rut their marriage has become. It's awkward, and it's uncomfortable, and it can be intimidating for a guy, but if they don't make the effort, their wives may start looking elsewhere to make them feel complete. It's up to men now."

There was a long silence. The only sound in the room was the scratch of Leticia's pen as it raced across the page of the notebook. She was frowning with concentration, trying to get down what I had said onto paper. I waited patiently until she looked back up at me. She flexed the fingers of her hand and smiled. "I'm guessing that happens to be a sore point with you?"

I nodded. "Sorry," I said. "I tend to go on."

"Have you had married women come to you, Jonah?" Leticia asked. "Do married women come to you and ask you to train them as submissives because their husbands won't – or can't – make the effort to give them this BDSM experience?"

"It's happened," I said vaguely.

"More than once?"

"Several times."

"What do you do? Do you take those women on as new submissives?"

"No. Not if I know they're married."

"Why not?"

"Because they're married women," I explained. "I encourage them to go back to their man and try again. And if they have already tried again, I would encourage them to try harder. It's easier to save their marriage through concerted, patient effort than it is to start all over again."

Leticia shook her head. "Surely if a woman has gone to her husband and shared her fantasies about BDSM with him, and he refuses to try to please her, then there's nothing more that can be done."

"Not true," I said. "The man simply needs to understand that he has to change his approach."

Leticia challenged me with raised eyebrows. "You're looking at the problem from the wrong side," I said. "The average man is intimidated by the whole BDSM fantasy. Why? I'll tell you why. Because they don't feel comfortable if it's something they're not familiar with when it comes to sex. So when the wife comes to the husband all breathless and excited because she has read a collection of erotic BDSM stories, he refuses. In her mind, the woman has the fantasy all played out. She's visualized the setting. She's visualized how the man of her dreams looks. She's imagined how the room will look – the sights, smells, and sounds. She can see herself tied to the bed with soft romantic lighting and rose petals scattered all around her. Her fantasy man blindfolds her, covers her with kisses, ties her hands together and ravages her. It's perfect – and no average husband can compete with that."

"My point exactly!" Leticia said.

"So the husband needs to do everything the woman fantasized about, but do it in a different location, and at a different time."

Silence. Leticia just sat staring at me in confusion.

I went on. "The fantasy the woman has in her head is impossible for her husband to re-create. It will always be a disappointment, because the fantasy is so perfect. So if she imagines these events happening of a nighttime in a bedroom, the husband needs to repeat them of a daytime in the kitchen. That way it becomes *their* shared fantasy, and he has no expectations to live up to. He can't fail – he can only produce a different, similar experience – but it will be one the woman will appreciate because he made the effort, and he made that moment theirs."

Leticia thought about that. She sat in the silence frowning and pursing her lips getting her head around the idea. She nodded grudgingly, as though just maybe the idea had merits after all, and then went back to her earlier question.

"So married women are off limits?"

"To me, yes. Maybe not to others, but they are to me. It's in the Jonah Noble big book of rules."

"What about boyfriends?"

"It's the same," I nodded. "Every woman in a committed relationship is off limits."

Leticia tilted her head to the side and studied me. "That's a strangely old-fashioned attitude..."

I shrugged. "It's my rule," I said. "It works for me. If I know a woman is in a committed relationship, they're off limits." And then I added, "Leticia, there are plenty of single, separated and divorced women in the world looking to explore their submissive fantasies with a Master. I don't need to get in the middle of a marriage."

"You mean women like Sherry?"

"Exactly," I said. "Sherry was naturally submissive. Remember, this was years before that book came out. It wasn't something that Sherry read about and decided she wanted to discover more. The need to submit sexually was something instinctive within her. When she came back to the office every Friday night after work, she was in a trembling state of arousal and anticipation."

Leticia looked thoughtful and then frowned. "How do you test the limits of someone who is a natural submissive?" she asked. "I mean, I understand if you have a new submissive who wants to explore BDSM submission to discover more about herself. But what if she already knows? What do you do when someone like Sherry comes to you, and she is already a willing submissive? How do you take that to the next level?"

"Good question," I smiled.

I started pacing again. "For the first few Friday nights, Sherry and I were simply in lust. I took her in every office in the building: bent over desks, or with her back pressed up against a wall and her dress down around her ankles. I laid her out on the front reception counter and slid down between her spread thighs, and I teased her mercilessly with my tongue and fingers. I made her beg for every orgasm she received, and I made her beg to suck my cock. I covered her with my body and felt her tiny heels digging into the back of my legs as she wrapped herself around me and writhed in orgasm. And I made her kneel before me and finger-fuck herself while she used her mouth to suck me to orgasm. She was insatiable.

"Then, one night, she asked me to hurt her."

Leticia balked. "Hurt her?"

I nodded, and then explained quickly. "Not pain for the sake of pain," I said. "Not cruelty. Sherry wanted to experience *exquisite* pain – the kind of sweet pain that is almost – but not quite – pleasure."

"Oh." Leticia sat back in the sofa and the sudden tension went out of her body. "So what did you do?"

"We talked about it," I said. "Sherry told me the idea of being tortured aroused her, but she had never been able to explore the fantasy because she feared being hurt. She didn't want the kind of torture that was typified by the idea of enduring unimaginable punishment or beatings. She wanted to feel strung out with the torture of needing to come, and being made to wait and wait until she felt she would explode."

"And you made that happen?"

I nodded and gave Leticia a wicked smile.

"The following Friday night I told Sherry to arrive at the office an hour later. I needed to prepare. It was the first time I had actually put thought and planning into a session with a submissive, and it was the first time I had ever used real props. In a way it was a significant moment in my journey towards becoming a BDSM Master."

"Props?" Leticia asked.

"Props and planning," I said. "They're two essential ingredients for BDSM," I explained. "There is only so much a Master can do without planning a session – not everything is spontaneous. And props – well a few items are essential in my opinion. I'm not advocating that your readers of this article spend thousands of dollars on equipment. I'm simply saying that a couple of items are handy to have."

"Such as?"

"A riding crop, or some kind of a whip, a blindfold, and a pair of handcuffs, or rope. They're my essentials. Some Masters like to intimidate submissives. They lead them into a dark gloomy room filled with leather and manacles and chains and whipping benches – but all that stuff is really just for show. It's not necessary for the average man looking to explore the BDSM lifestyle with his partner."

Leticia wrote everything down dutifully, and then flipped over to a new page. She shifted on the sofa, so that she was sitting upright with her knees pressed together and her feet on the floor. She looked up at me like a student about to be asked the first question of an important exam.

I had her attention and interest…

"When Sherry arrived at the office that evening, I led her downstairs to the production room. As I said before, it was really a converted underground garage. The floor was concrete and the walls makeshift. I had moved the production benches around to create a large table on one side of the room.

"Sherry came down the stairs and stopped suddenly in astonishment. I saw the look on her face – she was confused, but excited. I heard her gasp, and then a shiver ran through her body. She saw coiled lengths of rope on the table and she drifted towards them in a dream-like, hypnotic state. I snatched at her wrist and told her to undress. She was wearing a sweater and loose pants. She slid them off and stood in just a pair of red panties. I stood close behind her and felt her tremble. I pulled her hair away from her neck and bit her. Her knees buckled. 'You will not come tonight. Do you understand your Master?' Sherry nodded. Suddenly she was anxious. I reached my hand around and pinched one of her nipples hard. She gasped. 'I am going to use you for my pleasure this evening – your mouth and your pussy. You will give yourself to me and only to me. There will be no orgasm for you'.

"I took her by the hand and led her to the side of the table. I tied her wrists together. When I looked into Sherry's face she was panting in short agitated breaths. Her lips were parted and her eyes were wide and unblinking. She was incredibly aroused.

"I led her away from the bench and stood her in the middle of the floor. Then I tied an extra length of rope to her wrists and ran it through a ring-bolt that I had screwed into the ceiling. Sherry hadn't noticed it up until that moment. I pulled the rope so her wrists were suspended above her head and she was completely at my mercy."

Leticia's eyes were hunting mine. Her face was flushed. There was crimson color on her cheeks and in a rash across her throat. She had stopped writing. She was watching me, seeming to hang breathlessly on every word.

"I let Sherry dangle from the ceiling for a few moments, admiring the shape of her body, enjoying the vulnerability of her. I tied a silk scarf over her eyes as a blindfold and stood in front of her, keeping my voice low and even as I told her all the things she would be made to do that night. Sherry smiled at me through trembling lips. I squeezed her nipple again, tugging gently, and she let out a husky gasp.

"I had bought clothes pins. I sucked on her tiny breasts until both her nipples were jutting and firm, and then I placed a pin onto each of her nipples. Sherry flinched and cringed. She made a soft whimpering sound in the back of her throat. I flicked one of the pins with my fingers and Sherry went suddenly stiff as though she had been electrocuted. 'Do you like that?' I asked. Her mouth fell open, her jaw hung slack. Her lips were wet and glistening, and she groaned again.

"I didn't wait for an answer. I ran my hands down her stomach. A rash of little bumps sprang up along her arms. I slid my hand over the damp silk of her panties and pressed my palm hard against her mound. Sherry bucked her hips once, and then thrust herself forward urgently, rubbing and grinding herself against my hand. I let her. I let her writhe and squirm, hanging from the hook in the ceiling until I could tell that she was about to thrill. I pulled my hand away and she groaned aloud with a sound like a devastated ache. 'I told you not to come tonight,' I said. Sherry caught her breath and made a little sobbing sound. I pressed my hand back against the aching dampness of her pussy again and her whole body went stiff as she tried to resist her natural need to orgasm. I slid my fingers along her slit, pressing the damp fabric into the cleft of her pussy. She bit down on her lip. 'You're so fucking wet,' I marveled. 'I can feel the heat and the dampness of you.'

"I tugged at the elastic of her panties and she swung towards me, caught off balance. I hooked a finger down inside the waistband and tore them from her. I took the tattered shreds of her underwear and held them in my hand. 'Open your mouth'.

"Sherry obeyed. I pressed the panties between her lips and told her to suck her juices from them."

Leticia moved on the sofa like she was perched on the edge of a bed of nails. She was uncomfortable. She resettled herself. The color on her cheeks was a hectic flush.

"I had bought a riding crop from a local store," I said. I wasn't really looking at Leticia now. I was staring off into the distance, wandering rather than pacing, my memories vivid and all-consuming. "It was just a standard crop – nothing special. I swished it in the air and it made a wicked hissing sound. Sherry heard the new sound and winced.

"'You have displeased me,' I told Sherry. 'You've acted like a wanton little whore tonight. You were told this evening was about giving your Master pleasure, and yet you try to use me to give yourself an orgasm,' my voice was hard and harsh – the voice of a stranger, but it was all part of the scene. But Sherry didn't know that. 'I'm sorry,' she blurted. 'Please forgive me.'

"I cut the whip through the air again, and then went behind her. I drew out the seconds, building her anxiety. Then I traced the tip of the crop down her back. She arched her body, and the knuckles of her spine stood proud against her skin like a string of pale little pearls. I drew the whip down until it was sliding along the cleft of her clenched bottom and then rubbing back and forth along the moist gap between her parted thighs."

I stopped in mid-step and suddenly turned to Leticia, my eyes clear and focused, the memories set aside for an instant.

"Have you ever been whipped by a riding crop?"

Leticia looked at me with horror in her eyes. "Of course not!" she blushed.

I shrugged. "Well it hurts. It hurts like hell. A good cut of a riding crop will bring tears to a brave man's eyes. The pain is sharp and severe – so I was very careful with Sherry. I didn't want to cause her pain – and that wasn't the kind of pain she wanted me to introduce her to. So I lined the crop up with one of the taut cheeks of her bottom and tapped it – repeatedly, using short fast strokes from my wrist. Sherry flinched at the first touch of the crop, and then as I tapped her again and again in the same spot, a bright red flush of heat spread across her bottom. She balanced on one leg, swinging from the rope, trying to draw herself away from me. She shifted her weight, dancing from one foot to the other as though she were standing on hot coals – and all the while I kept lightly tapping the same spot on her bottom until she was whimpering softly and swaying on her arms.

"I stood back. Sherry's breathing was ragged. I knew the throbbing sting from the crop would be a lingering burn for some time. I told her she should thank her Master, and she did.

"'Good girl,' I said. Then I unfastened my pants. My cock was as hard as a length of iron bar. Sherry turned her head as if to look over her shoulder, even though she was blindfolded. She sensed what was coming. I saw the fine muscles of her calves and thighs flex as she spread her legs wider. I pressed myself hard against her and slid all the way inside the wet clenching warmth of her pussy.

"Sherry's head fell forward between her raised arms. I clamped my hands around her waist to hold her in place and thrust into her again and again. She was sobbing, trembling. She muttered words I couldn't understand like she was in the delirium of some fever. I felt the muscles in my chest and forearms seize tight, and I was snarling and growling through clenched teeth as each thrust became a shuddering impact.

"'Come!' I hissed in Sherry's ear suddenly. I was right on the edge of erupting. Every fiber of my body was strung tight, like a bow drawn and held by the archer for too long. The tremble of exertion spread from my legs and burned like fire. I heard Sherry gasp and cry out – and then she was writhing and spasming and swinging from the ropes, her whole body seized in violent convulsions. The sudden grasp and pulse of her was like a tight grip around the length of me. I lasted just an instant longer, and then felt the release of my own orgasm like the crash of a wave. I clung to Sherry, both of us spent and exhausted, both of us held upright by the rope in the ceiling. It was one of the most shattering orgasms of my life."

Leticia sat back, like she was drained just from hearing the story re-told. "You let Sherry have an orgasm after all."

"Of course," I said simply. "I had always intended to – I just didn't let her know. I didn't want her to take her own orgasms for granted. I wanted her to know that her pleasure was now under my control."

"It sounds like one heck of a night," Leticia said.

"It was," I agreed, "but that was just the start of it. I still haven't told you about the table and the rest of the rope."

Leticia stood up suddenly and came a couple of steps closer to me. "I need a break," she said. She disappeared down the hallway for several minutes and when she came back she had changed into faded old jeans and a soft pink top that buttoned down the front. I said nothing. Leticia went into the kitchen, and I watched the way her bottom moved in her jeans with appreciation. She glanced back over her shoulder at me, her eyes wide and bemused, like she knew I had been admiring her.

"Coffee?"

"Good idea," I said. I was suddenly weary. I eased myself into one corner of the tiny sofa and rubbed the knotted muscles at the back of my neck. There was the blunt, distant pulse of a headache beginning to throb behind my eyes.

Maybe I was drinking too much.

Maybe I wasn't drinking enough...

Leticia brought me a steaming mug of coffee. There was a smile on her face: a secret womanly smile that made her lips soft and moist. I leaned forward to take the cup in both hands and the top of her blouse gaped open. She wasn't wearing a bra. I caught a tantalizing glimpse of firm breast and ruby-red nipple. I sat back with the coffee. Leticia sauntered away into the kitchen. She was humming softly to herself. She picked up her own cup and stopped in the doorway. The bright light silhouetted her clearly: the curve of her hips and the narrowness of her waist.

"I have a question for you," I said. "Do you want me to ask it now, or after I tell you what I did with Sherry on the table?"

Leticia sipped at her coffee, and for a moment I thought she hadn't heard me. She seemed to be lost in some private secret thought. I waited.

"Finish the story with Sherry," she said softly. "You know how I hate to have my notes disorganized."

I set my cup down on the small table and rubbed my eyes. They felt gritty.

"I untied Sherry from the hook, but left her wrists bound," I began, picking up the story as though returning to an open page of a book. "I took the blindfold off. She blinked at me. Her panties had fallen from her mouth when she had orgasmed. I left them where they had fallen and led Sherry over to the table. She stood, wide-eyed and panting. Her legs were trembling so that she could hardly stand. I took the pins from her nipples and for a moment, there was an expression of blessed relief on her face. Then the blood raced back into her breasts, and she contorted in exquisite pain – like the pain you feel when you have pins and needles, and you stomp your foot to get the blood flowing again. It was like that – only the intensity amplified because of the sensitivity of her nipples. Sherry writhed. I held her bound wrists and watched her face.

"I laid her out on the table on her back and moved her body so that her hips were resting on the edge. I held her legs apart and raised them high. Her pussy was wide open and exposed to me, glistening with the damp juices of sex.

"I was already hardening again. I stepped up to the edge of the table and rested my cock against the lips of her pussy. Sherry's legs were against my chest, her tiny heels pressed against my shoulders. I eased myself inside her and felt the tight grip of her body like an involuntary reflex. I held myself still and Sherry's muscles pulsed and sent quivering vibrations down the length of my shaft.

"She turned her head to the side and closed her eyes. I could see a frown of concentration on her face. She trapped her bottom lip between her teeth, as though she were riding the gentle swells of sensation.

"'Fuck me,'' I said. 'Use your muscles to fuck your Master.'

"Sherry screwed her eyes tight and began to make little sobbing sounds of effort. I felt the muscles within her clench, and the grip around the swelling head of my cock was tight and firm. It lasted for just a few seconds and then released. I heard Sherry give a little gasp as though she had been holding her breath.

"'Again!' I barked at her. I closed my own eyes and concentrated on the feel of her clenching pussy – the way her inner body seized tight. With each new command, I felt myself hardening inside her. A dozen times I ordered her to milk my cock with her muscles. Sherry began to sweat. A glossy sheen of perspiration spread across her breasts, and she began to pant as if she had run up a hill. The muscles in her neck strained, and she turned her head from one side to the other. I reached down and rubbed the nub of her clit with my thumb and she flinched with the tiny shock of it. Her whole sex throbbed, and a sudden groan of desire was wrenched from her throat. Her eyes came open, but her expression was dull and dream-like. I told her to pleasure herself while I fucked her, and her hands went between her spread legs.

"I started to thrust deep inside her. Having her legs in the air and her body in that position meant she felt the full length of me deep inside her. Our bodies slammed together and Sherry began to rock her hips. The muscles of her abdomen stood proud, like little ridges against the firm skin, and her hands between her legs became a blur. It was difficult for her: with her wrists still bound, her fingers couldn't quite touch the places she wanted to in the way she desperately needed, to reach orgasm. She made little grunting sounds of frustration between gasps of pleasure, and I felt my own body beginning to grow tight with rising tension as the urge to explode inside her again became a hungry need."

Suddenly I needed to stand. I got up from the sofa and scraped my hands down my face. The headache, which had been crouched in the darkness behind my eyes, finally pounced. I winced. My vision blurred and little swirling flashes of light floated before my eyes.

"Are you okay?" Leticia's face was uncertain.

I nodded. I needed another drink, but the wine bottle was empty.

I closed my eyes, stood still for a moment, and then continued with the story, my voice lower now and sounding in my own ears almost trance-like.

"I told Sherry she had until the count of ten to come. I told her that if she couldn't come by then, she would be sent home for the weekend without relief. I meant it. Her eyes flashed with horror. Her face became a mask of frantic desperation. Her fingers flew across her clit, and at the same time I dug my own fingers into the muscled flesh of her legs to give me leverage. I lunged into her, thrusting from my hips as I stared down at the way her tiny breasts jiggled and the hard urgency of her nipples.

"I started counting. Sherry arched her back, trying to get herself off. She became more desperate. Her body contorted like she was on a torturer's rack. Her voice rose until the sounds of sex filled the room. I felt myself beginning to thrill. Sherry was rigid beneath me. She gave one last cry of frustration, and then suddenly her body seemed to catch fire and she was wrenched from side to side as her orgasm battered and bashed through her body.

"The fierce convulsions within her sent me over the edge," I said softly. "I pulled my cock from her pussy and wrapped my hand around Sherry's throat, pinning her flat on the table. I rubbed my cock against her lips, and her mouth opened instinctively. I forced her mouth closed again. Sherry had a split second to open her eyes in confusion – and then suddenly I erupted across her face: covering her cheek and chin.

"For a long time there was nothing apart from the emptiness. We were both gasping for breath. Sherry lay like a broken doll on the table, her legs dangling, her body still twisted, and I leaned over her, feeling the thumping pulse of blood singing in my ears.

"When my senses cleared – when everything was quiet again – I told Sherry she was to dress and go home. I told her to leave my come on her face: she was not to wash it off until the next morning. For a moment she hesitated – and then nodded obediently. I knew she had a roommate. I knew she shared a little apartment with another girl, but I didn't care."

"Did she?" Leticia asked in a hushed voice. "I mean, did she leave.... until the next morning?"

I shrugged. "I can't be sure," I admitted. "But knowing Sherry, and knowing what happened the following Friday night, it's a pretty safe bet that she did."

"What do you mean?" There was that sudden tone of scandal in her voice I had heard before, as though some shocking secret might be revealed. "What happened the following Friday night?"

I shook my head. "I can't begin to tell you," I said slyly. "It's too late in the night to begin that story – and I know how you hate having your notes disjointed..."

Leticia made a face.

"Besides, now you have to answer my question. Remember?"

She did, but clearly, she had hoped I'd forgotten. Leticia's shoulders slumped, as though she had just been told bad news. She gave a little nod of her head.

"You better sit down for this one," I teased.

Her expression became wary and concerned. She sat on the sofa. She crossed her legs and folded her arms across her chest. I started to pace. The headache suddenly spiked, and then began to fade to a dull throb.

"Have you ever thought about BDSM?" I asked. "Have you ever fantasized about what it would be like to submit your mind and your body to a Master?"

"No," Leticia shook her head, and it was an adamant gesture with no hesitation. "Not once have I ever even considered the idea," she went on – and then paused dramatically, "...until I met you. Now... now it seems to be the only thing I can think about." Her voice trailed off and there was a heavy wistful silence.

I didn't say anything for a long time.

I didn't know what to say.

I started pacing again. "If you were a submissive, and if you served a Master, what would your soft limits be?" I asked.

"Soft limits?"

I nodded. "Soft limits. What would you submit yourself to willingly, and what things would you consider, without committing yourself to?"

Leticia looked flustered. Her hands fluttered and then settled in her lap. She glanced around the room like she was looking for a way to escape.

"I… I don't know," she mused softly. "I really haven't thought about it."

"Then do it now," I insisted. I prompted her. "Would you have sex with another woman while your Master watched?"

"Um… I don't know," she wrung her hands.

I went on. "Would you allow yourself to be tied?"

"Yes."

"Would you allow yourself to be handcuffed or chained?"

"Yes. I think so," her voice was low – nothing more than a soft breathless whisper.

"Would you have sex with another man while your Master watched?"

She shook her head.

"Would you allow yourself to be blindfolded?"

"Yes," her voice was a little firmer.

"What about being spanked? Would you bend yourself over your Master's knee for a spanking if you deserved punishment?"

"If it was deserved… yes…"

"And whipped, maybe with a riding crop?"

Leticia winced. "If I trusted the man, and if it was deserved."

I was pacing around the room, firing questions to the beat of my footsteps like a sergeant major on a parade ground filled with fresh-faced army recruits. I clasped my hands behind my back and circled the room, Leticia's head turning on the long graceful stem of her neck to follow me with her eyes.

"Would you wear a Master's collar in public?"

Leticia hesitated. "I don't know," she confessed. "I know a submissive is supposed to be proud of her collar. I know it's like a wedding ring because it's a sign of commitment – but I'm standing on the outside looking in, Jonah. I don't know how I would feel if I was living the lifestyle," she shrugged and grimaced at the same time. "So I just can't answer that question."

I nodded and thought for a moment. "Have you wondered how it would feel to wear a collar?"

"Yes."

"And…?"

Leticia sighed and looked thoughtful. "I imagine it would make me feel a lot of different things," she speculated. "I imagine being collared would be a source of pride – a sign that I was skilled and obedient and competent enough to be wanted by someone. I guess I would also feel confident," the tone of her voice lifted so that the comment almost became a question. She shrugged. "I'm only guessing," she said to qualify her words. "I don't think anyone really knows, except for a submissive woman who is already collared. And maybe it's different for every woman. Maybe submission means something different to me than it does to women who are already immersed in the lifestyle."

The depth of her reasoning, and the way she expressed herself surprised me. I was very much aware of her age and her inexperience, and I had expected her answers to be filled with giddy little giggles and blushing immaturity. But her replies demonstrated how much thought she had given to the subject since I had met her, and how well she knew herself – and perhaps her own limitations.

"Do you think you could give up your right to have an orgasm whenever you wanted, and pass that responsibility over to a Master?" I asked Leticia.

"You mean only orgasm when he permitted me to?"

"Yes."

She frowned. "I guess so..." she said tentatively. "If I was comfortable in the role of a submissive, and if I felt it was a necessary part of the whole kind of learning process."

"Learning process? You mean learning about yourself?"

"Yes," Leticia said, and then looked up earnestly into my face. "Isn't that what submission is really all about, Jonah? Isn't it a way for a woman to discover and learn something new about herself – maybe something that she never realized was a primal part of her?"

I smiled. "It is," I said. "That's exactly what I believe submission is, and that's exactly what I believe a good Master does. He gives a woman the chance to discover herself."

There was another long silence – but this one was different. It wasn't the awkward quiet of embarrassment, nor was it the reflective silence that I was prone to lapse into.

It was a significant silence – as though something had just changed – some realization or deeper connection of understanding had just been made. It lasted for several minutes. Finally I roused myself. I was tired. My headache came snarling back from the dull recesses, and clamped tight above my eyes like a steel band.

At her front door, Leticia put a sudden hand on my arm. Her skin was warm. "Tomorrow is the weekend," she said. "I don't have to work."

I nodded. "I understand. How about you call me on Monday and we can make a time to continue with the interview then."

"No," she said quickly. "You don't understand. I didn't mean it like that. I meant… I meant I had the weekend free and I was wondering if you liked parks?"

I was puzzled. "Parks? The ones with green grass and trees?"

"Uhuh."

"I remember them," I made my voice sound vague.

Leticia gave a little smile. "Well there is a park near here I would like to take you to. It's a place I like to go to when I have things to think through – stuff to sort out. I'd like to show it to you – if you're not too busy." She smiled for a moment like she was being silly and then looked steadily into my eyes, compelled suddenly to explain.

"When I first moved here, I had no friends – I barely even knew the people at the newspaper," Leticia said softly. "So I went to the park. The city was so busy, so loud. I wasn't used to the hustle and bustle. I'm from a small town and I had a hard time adjusting to the frenetic pace of everyone around me. The park reminded me of home. It was my little sanctuary away from all the chaos..."

I smiled. "Okay, I'm sold," I said and held up my hands in mock surrender. "And I'm sure a few hours in the fresh air and sunshine won't kill me."

* * *

It rained in the morning and then the clouds burned away and the sun came blazing down.

Leticia met me in the foyer of her apartment building at midday, and we walked the few blocks to the park. A muggy, steamy smell rose from the sidewalk as the heat baked the rain off the concrete.

It was the first time Leticia had seen me in just a t-shirt and denim jeans. She said nothing, but I noticed the glances from the corner of her eye.

The park was a square block of vibrant green lawns in the heart of the city, bordered on every side by busy roads, yet protected from the snarl of traffic by tall lush trees that stood like a dense fringe of sentinels.

An overhead bridge stretched across an inner-city street and we climbed to the top and stood for a moment, leaning on the safety rail. Directly below us, the traffic streamed in both directions beneath a haze of fumes and smog. Behind us, the city office blocks were towers of reflective glass – and ahead was an Eden of green tranquility, with kids and families enjoying the blue afternoon sky.

We went down the footbridge steps and onto a meandering path that wound its way through a stone archway and into the park.

There were benches and tables scattered around the edges of the open space beneath tall shady trees, and the grass was a green carpet of gentle undulations.

Leticia led me to a park bench, and I could hear the sound of ducks and splashing water somewhere nearby. I sat down under the dappled shade of a tree and Leticia sat beside me. She was wearing a pale yellow dress that reached to her knees. She tucked the hem neatly beneath her and then swung her legs playfully, like a child on a swing set. I took a deep breath – the air was somehow fresher here, and the sun had a crystal kind of clarity away from the haze of city smog.

"Beautiful, isn't it."

I nodded. "It really is," I said.

A dozen yards away a man was walking his dog, and a young woman in tight lycra pants and a 49ers sweat shirt went jogging past. Leticia reached into her bag for a pair of sunglasses and perched them on the end of her nose. I noticed her notebook tucked into a corner of the bag.

"Tell me about your family," I said. "Did you get along with your mother and father?"

Leticia made a thoughtful face. "I guess so," she said. "I was always daddy's girl. I spent a lot of time with him when I was younger – not so much when I reached my teens and started high school. But we were always close. I could always talk to him."

"But not your mother?"

Leticia shook her head. "Not so much," she admitted frankly. "Mom got kind of distant after she lost her job in one of the local stores. Dad had to pick up extra shifts at the processing plant, and mom started drinking in the afternoons... and into the evenings. She kind of faded away out of my life for a while. Do you know what I mean?"

I nodded. "I think so," I said. "But what about now? Are you in regular contact with your folks?"

Leticia nodded. "I call once a week, but there isn't a lot to say. We don't have anything to share, unless it's gossip from around the town. That takes a minute or two, and then we just hang on the phone for ten awkward minutes until I feel like I've done my duty as a daughter and can hang up."

I didn't probe further. I sensed there was more to the story, but it was clear that Leticia's family were not a big part of her life, and she seemed okay with that.

A couple of kids were throwing a baseball, tossing the ball in a high lazy arc to each other. The sound of the ball thudding into catcher's mitts reminded me of my own childhood.

I got up from the bench and wandered around on the grass. I sensed Leticia's eyes on me behind the dark lenses of her sunglasses. She watched me for a while, saying nothing – both of us aware of each other and comfortable in the silence.

"Do you read much?" Leticia asked me suddenly. "I saw your library, but some people just like books – they don't like reading."

I nodded. "I used to read a lot," I said. "Mainly historical fiction."

"You mean those breathless romantic bodice rippers?"

"No," I started to smile. "I mean *good* historical fiction."

She asked me if I had favorite authors and I mentioned the names of several. "How about you?"

Leticia took off her sunglasses. "Well lately all the reading I've done has been about the BDSM lifestyle."

"Oh? Fact or fiction?"

Leticia gestured with a tilt of her head and a shrug of her shoulders. "Both," she said. "Online articles and some mainstream erotica."

There was another pause of amiable silence. I stuffed my hands into the pockets of my jeans and kicked at a tuft of grass. "Don't romanticize the lifestyle, Leticia," I said. "Don't build it up in your mind to be something that it isn't. BDSM isn't the solution to every relationship in trouble, it's not the answer for every lonely girl looking for love, and it's not all about charming doms and beautiful breathless subs. And please," I said with sudden intensity, "please don't romanticize my story when you write it. I'm being honest with you, and you should be honest with your readers. For every erotic encounter I have detailed, there have been just as many failures – times when things didn't work the way I planned, or wanted. Just tell it like it is. Be honest. Make sure you know the difference between being a reporter of the facts and a writer who is trying to titillate and entertain."

Leticia stared at me and nodded slowly. "I know the difference," she said, sounding defensive. "But you're Jonah Noble. You're larger than life. You can't expect people to believe your story is ordinary. It's not – and neither are you."

The irony. I was warning Leticia about the realities of BDSM, and she was defending me against my own criticism.

"When you strip all the props, the imagery, the erotica and the mystery away, BDSM is about two people, trying to discover what makes them happy in life – what gives them a sense of belonging and completion. The rest is just tinsel on the tree. It's all decoration."

Leticia looked shocked. "You sound very cynical."

"I'm not trying to be," I said sincerely. "I just know from experience that expectations are hard to live up to."

"What happened that following Friday night with Sherry?" Leticia asked, changing the subject with all the subtlety of a wrecking ball.

I shrugged. I had tried.

"She brought her roommate along for the evening," I said.

“Huh?” Leticia wasn’t paying attention. She was digging into her handbag for her notebook and a pen.

“I said she brought her roommate along. They were both standing at the door waiting for me when I went back to the office after dinner.”

Leticia’s head snapped round. “The roommate was there? Holy shit! Did you know that was going to happen?”

“I did. Sherry spoke to me during the week. She said she had told her roommate all about us. She said her friend wanted to know if she could come along and watch.”

“And you said yes.”

I nodded.

“Why?”

“Why not?” I shrugged.

“What happened?”

I started to pace around the bench, but it wasn’t working for me. Strangely, not being hemmed in by walls made my pacing redundant. So I stood with my hands in my pockets and stared up at the treetops as my mind was drawn back to that night all those years earlier.

“The roommate’s name was Denella. She was the physical opposite of Sherry. She was a tall girl with long brown hair. But where Sherry’s body was slim and almost child-like, Denella had a much different figure. She was eight inches taller than Sherry, with large heavy breasts and wide womanly hips.

“I had never met her. She was nervous. I walked straight up to her and kissed her fiercely, and at the same time I cupped one of her breasts possessively in my hand. Denella went rigid with shock for about five seconds, and then suddenly the tension went from her body. Her lips parted for me, and I slid my tongue into her mouth. I reached inside her blouse and lifted one breast from within the cup of her bra. Her nipple was hard, and her breasts had weight and substance to them. The skin was incredibly soft, and I massaged and kneaded the warm flesh until I heard her give a little gasp of pleasure."

"What was Sherry doing?"

"Watching," I said. "The day before Denella arrived I had asked Sherry if they were lovers. She said they weren't. She said they had talked about the idea of having sex together, but had decided not to take the chance on risking their friendship."

"Did you believe Sherry?"

"Yes," I said. "And I think if they had been lovers Sherry would have joined in when I was standing kissing her roommate. It was the perfect opportunity for the whole session to become some crazy threesome – but Sherry simply stood back and watched me take Denella like it was my right."

"What happened next?"

"I took the girls to my office. I unbuttoned Denella's blouse and unfastened her bra. Then I lifted her skirt. She had wide hips, so I hoisted it as high as I could and told her to spread her legs. She didn't say a word. She simply did as I told her. She was wearing white lace panties. I stared her in the eye, fixing her with my gaze, and then I rubbed her pussy through her panties."

"Just like that?"

I nodded.

"And you had never met this woman before in your life?"

I shook my head.

"And she let you undress her and... and arouse her – without saying a word?"

"That's right," I said. "But she was Sherry's roommate. No doubt Sherry had told her what to expect, and what she might need to do if she wanted to join in for the night. It's not like she was a complete stranger off the street, and it's not like she didn't know what was going to happen that night."

Leticia looked at me like maybe I had super powers, and then shook her head in bewilderment. She wrote something down into the margin of her notebook and then underlined it several times with big heavy lines. She looked up at me expectantly. "Well you can't stop now! What happened with Denella?"

"I told her to take off her skirt and blouse, and then I turned and ordered Sherry to undress. Denella wriggled out of her clothes but left her panties on. She was trembling – not scared, just excited. I stood close to her and rubbed her mound again through her panties. 'Tell me why you're here tonight,' I asked her. She said she wanted to watch. I told her to call me sir. She said Sherry had told her some of the ways I had used her, and she wanted to watch. Then she added, 'sir'.

"I stepped back. Sherry was naked. I ordered her onto her knees, and then told her to take Denella's panties off – with her teeth."

Leticia looked up from her notebook, then back down again. Her hand raced across the page.

"Do you want me to slow down?"

Leticia shook her head. Didn't say anything. She was frowning as she wrote, maybe trying to get it all down on paper and keep the words assembled in her head. I tried pacing again, but it just felt stupid. I went back to staring at the trees.

"Sherry crawled across to Denella, and the two girls started giggling. I slapped Sherry's perfect little ass, and the laughter stopped. She got her teeth on the waistband of Denella's panties and began to tug them down."

"What did Denella do?"

"She stood there."

"What did you do?"

"I sat back in the chair and watched. Sherry struggled for a couple of minutes and Denella turned bright red with embarrassment, and maybe a little arousal. Finally she was able to step out of her panties, and Sherry sat back on her haunches, a little breathless."

"Was Sherry aroused?"

"I think so. The two girls had discussed having sex together, so there was some physical attraction between them. That's why I ordered Sherry to take Denella's panties of with her teeth. I wanted to test that attraction and see how Sherry reacted. I think, in different circumstances, they could easily have gotten into each other."

"But you didn't make that happen?"

"No," I said. "Denella told me she wanted to watch. So that was the experience I set about creating. I got out of the chair and told Denella to finger-fuck herself. She looked at me, and suddenly she wasn't giggling any more. Suddenly it all became very sexual and serious. She slid her hand down to her pussy, and I think the fact that Sherry was watching with wide excited eyes made it more difficult than if it had just been Denella and me in the room. She closed her eyes and began to rub her clit. When I had seen enough, I ordered her to stop."

"Seen enough?"

I nodded. "She was right handed. She used her fingers to tease herself. When I saw that, I told her to sit in my chair and play with herself while she watched me fuck Sherry. Then I told her the one condition."

Leticia looked up suddenly. "Which was…?"

"I told her she could only use her left hand."

Leticia stared at me for a moment with narrowed sly eyes. "That was cruel."

I nodded. "Very," I admitted. "In fact it's the kind of exquisite little exercise in BDSM and frustration that any woman can experiment with on her own in her own home."

Leticia paused. Her hand hovered above the page. She glanced up at me, maybe sensing that to ask a question now would divert me from retelling the encounter with Sherry and Denella – but she was curious. She couldn't help herself.

"What do you mean?"

"I mean that if a woman wanted a tame little insight into the lifestyle, she could always find a leather belt and fasten the hand they masturbate with to the headboard of their bed. Then they can try to pleasure themselves with their other hand."

"What would that do?"

"Just give a tiny little glimpse into some of the emotions they might feel and sensations they might experience if they were involved in a very gentle BDSM scene," I said. "Being bound and restrained is a turn on for a lot of women, and so is the feel of leather against their skin. Having their wrist bound above their head on the bed means they can get the sensation of being restrained, and at the same time the frustration of being aroused and wanting to orgasm – but not quite being able to reach the places they want in the way they are comfortable with." I shrugged.

Leticia didn't write any of that down, but she listened attentively and her expression became thoughtful. I had the feeling she was visualizing the idea, but she asked no more questions and I went back to that night with Sherry and Denella.

"Denella started to rub and finger her pussy," I said. "I bent Sherry over the edge of the desk and told her to spread her legs. I wanted to be sure Denella got the full sense of the experience. Dragging Sherry away to the far side of my office would make the whole incident too detached. I wanted it to be in Denella's face."

Leticia put her hand up suddenly like she was in school, and wanted the teacher's attention.

"You were still dressed?"

"Yes," I said. I suppressed the little flare of annoyance at being interrupted. "I waited until Sherry was leaning over the edge of the desk. She had her head lowered, but I could tell she was watching Denella pleasure herself. The two women were just a couple of feet apart. If Sherry had wanted to, she could have leaned across the desk and suckled one of Denella's nipples into her mouth. They were that close.

"I unfastened my belt, making sure Sherry heard the buckle being slipped and the zipper of my pants. It was part of the anticipation. Sex is a sensory thing for women. Sounds and scents are just as important as the other senses. For men it's all visual, but women are more complex. I wanted Sherry to know that I was undressing. I wanted her to imagine me standing behind her, and think about how exposed and open and vulnerable she was to me. I wanted to feel like she was at my mercy before I even laid a hand on her.

"I wrapped my hand around the buckle of the belt and used the soft end like a strap across Sherry's ass. The leather made a loud *'crack'* as it flicked across the firm pale flesh of her bottom. Sherry flinched and then I heard her gasp softly with arousal. I asked her if she wanted more, and she lowered her face to the tabletop and thrust out her butt in silent answer. I took the belt to her again, this time leaving a soft red line across her flesh."

"Were you punishing her?" Leticia asked.

"No, of course not," I said irritably. "I wasn't even trying to hurt her." I paused and took a deep breath. A young couple were spreading out a blanket on the grass nearby. I watched them for a moment.

"Leticia, just because I was using a belt on Sherry's ass, doesn't automatically mean I'm punishing or trying to hurt. Feeling the sting of a leather strap – if done correctly – can be a completely erotic sensation. Whips and belts and riding crops aren't just brutal ways to inflict pain. They should be props to heighten a submissive's arousal. That's what I was doing with Sherry. It's the difference between a sexy spanking and a beating. This was sexy spanking – with a leather belt. That's all."

Leticia nodded. "I get it," she said softly.

I had lost my train of thought. That happens when I'm interrupted. I stood moodily brooding for a few moments. The young couple had brought a picnic basket of food. The guy stretched out on his back and stared up at the sun while the woman set about unpacking the basket.

"My cock was hard," I said at last, and Leticia bowed her head back over the notebook. "I locked my hands around Sherry's hips to hold her still and she sucked in a short ragged breath of anticipation. Then I slid myself inside her, and there was a sudden rush of damp arousal as her excitement that had been welling between her thighs suddenly flowed over.

"I pushed myself deeply inside Sherry. It wasn't romance. It was sex. I wanted her to feel as though she was being dominated, that she was surrendering herself to me and that I was taking her – not making love to her. She grunted and groaned with every thrust of my cock, and the sounds of our bodies slamming together became louder. Sherry's fingers clawed desperately for the edge of the desk to support herself. She began to whimper and then push back with her hips to anticipate my next lunge. I leaned over her back and grabbed a fistful of her hair. I tugged, and she arched her back. She hissed in husky excitement.

"I still had the belt. I wrapped it around Sherry's throat and slipped the tail of leather through the buckle so it was hanging like a loose collar around her neck. The leather swished across the tabletop like a cat's tail as I pulled Sherry back onto my cock and began to thrust faster.

"Denella was watching me with huge, dazed eyes. Her fingers were glistening wet with her own juices and the lips of her sex were flared wide and open. She was tugging and pinching at her nipples with her right hand, and crying out softly in frustration. Her expression was ravenous.

"I felt myself beginning to thrill. My cock became impossibly hard. I felt the urge to explode become almost irresistible, and at the very last moment, I stopped thrusting and held myself still, deep inside Sherry. I felt a sudden pulse – a white-hot surge – and Sherry's pussy seemed to clamp tight around me as though trying to draw me deeper inside her. I screwed my eyes tightly shut and the room became suddenly quiet – like the calm before the storm. I was sweating. Beads of perspiration clung in my hair and trickled down my temple. I dug my fingers into the milky white flesh of Sherry's shoulders and she made a throaty sensuous sound. She was trembling. Her breathing was short and shallow little gasps. Denella had thrown one leg over the armrest of my chair so I could see the wet pink opening of her, glistening with the slick juice of her excitement.

"I waited for the moment to pass –maybe ten seconds – and then I thrust back into Sherry. The force of my lunge took her by surprise. Her legs buckled. I felt the strength go from her knees so that she lay like a rag doll, and I covered her body with mine so that my weight pressed her against the tabletop.

"Denella threw her head back suddenly and her mouth fell open. She was panting. Her fingers between her legs were a blur. Her whole body seemed drawn and tense. I could see the strain in her neck and the soft swell of her throat as she gulped and gasped.

"I forced myself faster and harder into Sherry's prone body. She was limp beneath me, totally passive and pliant. I clawed my way back to the brink of orgasm quickly and I clenched my jaw and hissed at the girls to come.

"Then it didn't matter. Then nothing mattered. My whole body seemed to catch fire and I felt the force of my orgasm erupt."

A couple of birds dropped down out of the trees and perched themselves on the edge of the park bench, like maybe they expected Leticia to feed them. I glanced away. It looked like the young couple sitting on the blanket were squabbling. The guy sat upright and gave a brusque shake of his head. The woman started cramming food back into the basket.

"Did Sherry and Denella... did they climax?" Leticia asked.

I turned back. "Sherry did, but not Denella. I asked her if she wanted help, but she seemed perfectly satisfied to be left frustrated – if that makes sense.

"I told the girls to dress and then sent them home."

Leticia tucked her notebook into her bag, and then asked me as an afterthought, "Did Denella join you and Sherry again after that first time? Did she become another submissive for you?"

"No," I said. "I never saw Denella again. In fact I was only at the newspaper for another couple of months, before I was forced to hand the day-to-day running of the business onto a manager."

"Oh? Why?" She started to reach for her notebook again.

"That was the time when I found out my father was ill," I explained. "I had to fly back home and become more involved with the overall business. We didn't know how much longer he would live."

"So you left Sherry behind?"

"Yes."

"Do you ever think about her?"

"Sometimes."

"Do you ever wish you had stayed in contact, or maybe brought her back here with you?"

"No."

"Why?"

That was a good question. I had asked myself the same thing a thousand times in the ensuing years.

"Because part of what made the time with Sherry special was the unspoken understanding between us that it would never be anything more than sex," I said. "There was never any talk of a relationship, and certainly never any talk about her becoming a full-time submissive to me. We just enjoyed the times we had together, and the roles we fell into. There was never a plan, and never a desire to commit – from me, or from her. It was what it was," I said simply, "and that's all it ever could have been."

* * *

We walked slowly back to Leticia's apartment and stood outside on the sidewalk in the afternoon sun. Traffic had thinned, but still the sounds of the city were a constant buzzing drone in the background. Leticia started towards the sliding glass doors, and then realized I wasn't beside her. She turned back to me and frowned.

"You aren't coming upstairs?"

I shook my head, staring at her with my hands thrust deep into the pockets of my jeans. "I want you to come to my place tonight," I said. "Eight o'clock."

Leticia arched her eyebrow and raised her chin in a little gesture of defiance. "And what if I have plans? It's Saturday night."

"Break them," I said, and my expression was serious. "There are some things I want to show you."

* * *

Trigg was waiting for me when I walked through the door. She stood in the foyer, her expression dark and brooding. Her eyes were slanted and narrowed into bright little blades, snapping with suppressed anger. I brushed past her. Her mouth was drawn into a grim line and words seemed to boil on her lips.

"Do you know what you're doing?" Trigg's voice was low and quivering.

I stopped in mid-stride. "It's not your concern," I said. "Let it be."

She followed me, light on her feet as a dancer, the sound of her heels on the tiles echoing against the high ceiling. She was dressed in black pants and a pink silk blouse. I could see a flush of angry color rise from beneath the shimmering fabric to her throat, and sense her bitterness.

Trigg caught her breath with a frustrated little hiss. "It's wrong, Jonah. You can't lead that young woman on like this."

I turned on her then, my voice crackled like breaking ice. "Don't tell me what to do," I warned. "It is none of your business," I said. "None."

Trigg took a startled step back. I stared into her eyes, a direct trail of strength. She dropped her gaze, and I went on while the anger still simmered and fizzed in my blood.

"Leticia is coming here tonight. She will arrive at eight o'clock. You will not be here. I don't care where you go for the evening, and I don't care what you do. But you will not be here. Do I make myself clear?"

Trigg nodded, suddenly uncertain. I left her standing alone, staring down at the floor, and stalked off towards the stairs.

* * *

The afternoon passed quickly. I sat at the big desk in my office and tried to concentrate. There was business to attend to. Muffled sounds from downstairs distracted me, and I went to the office door and found myself listening to Trigg's voice, talking on the telephone as she strode back and forth across the tiled floor.

I couldn't hear what she was saying, but I didn't need to. The tone in her voice was bitter and frustrated.

At six o'clock Mrs. Hortez brought a silver tray and left it on a small side-table just inside the door. We made polite, awkward conversation for a few seconds and then she left for the evening.

I returned my attention to the paperwork littered across the desk, but still I could not concentrate. I pushed the chair back and began to pace the floor, stopping once to listen to the crunch of tires and the steady burble of a car engine in the driveway. I went to the window and saw Trigg's convertible pulling out through the gates, the headlights bobbing and dipping as the vehicle merged into traffic and raced away into the darkening night.

I was alone. The house was eerie and silent.

Alone…

I began to pace once more, and suddenly it occurred to me that I was lonely. The realization was so shocking and disturbing that it stopped me in my tracks.

Being alone was something that I had always been comfortable with. I liked answering to no one. I enjoyed the freedom that came from remaining removed from emotional attachment. I had lived my life as my own man.

My world. My way.

It was the Jonah Noble battle-cry. But now, as I prowled back and forth across the floor, it struck me suddenly that I wasn't merely alone.

I was lonely.

Things: property and possessions surrounded me – and that had included the many women who had passed through my life; they had all been property to own, or possessions to entertain and arouse.

I went to the desk and swept all the paperwork into a drawer. I poured whisky into a glass and dropped into the big chair. The leather creaked and groaned around me.

I sat staring moodily at the darkened walls and wondered whether I had been playing the game of life to win, or merely not to get hurt from losing.

* * *

Leticia arrived a few minutes before eight o'clock. I had changed my t-shirt for a dress shirt, and my hair was still wet from a shower.

I pulled the front door open and she stood on the step wearing a short black skirt, heels and a soft grey blouse that buttoned down the front and was cut low enough to reveal a hint of tight cleavage. She smiled up at me, and I was enveloped in a soft subtle cloud of her perfume.

"You're right on time," I said.

She came through the door and stood in the foyer. I noticed she had changed handbags.

"Did you bring your notebook?"

She nodded. She looked around, as though she expected furniture to have been moved, or the house re-decorated. "It's very quiet," Leticia said. "Are we alone?"

"Yes," I said. "It's just you and me."

There was a moment of heavy silence, as though those words were significant. Leticia turned so that we were standing close to each other.

"You intrigued me today," she said softly. "The way you spoke in front of the apartment. It was all very mysterious."

I shrugged. "I didn't mean it to be," I said. "It's just that there are things you need to be shown so you can write the full story. Up until now I have told you about a couple of women from my distant past that helped shape my attitude towards the BDSM lifestyle. I figured now it was time to talk about my more recent past – and in order to do that, I need to show you a room."

"A room?"

I nodded. "The one next to my bedroom upstairs."

Leticia seemed to shiver. Her eyes were wide and unblinking. "Lead the way," she said breathlessly.

* * *

I unlocked the door and pushed it open. Leticia stepped across the threshold, and the disappointment on her face and in her body language was almost comical. She turned back and looked a puzzled question at me.

"This is the room you wanted to show me?"

"Yes."

It was a normal room, with an adjoining internal door that connected it to my own bedroom and a window set into the far wall. The room was sparsely furnished; there was an antique chest of drawers on one side, and an old dressing table next to it, with a large oval mirror. On the back wall – on either side of the window – were a couple of waist-high wooden shelves, and in the middle of the carpeted floor was a table and a chair.

The light in the ceiling was shaded, and there was a dimmer switch on the doorframe. I turned the dial to make the room a little brighter.

"This is it?" Leticia asked again.

"Yes," I said simply.

She let the strap of her handbag slip from her shoulder and walked towards the table. She set the handbag down on the floor beside the chair and walked a slow circuit of the room, the sound of her footsteps the only noise in the house.

She went to the window and drew the drapes apart. There was a view that stretched back into the distant hills, but all she saw was darkness. She let the drapes fall back into place and turned.

"What makes this room so special?"

"It's where I punish, discipline and train my submissives."

Leticia almost chuckled. "You're joking – right?"

I didn't move. "Look at my face, Leticia. Do I look like I'm joking?"

I was deadly serious.

Leticia frowned. "I'm sorry, Jonah, but I... well I expected something totally different. I mean, you're *Jonah Noble*, for heaven's sake. Shouldn't you have some dark gloomy dungeon in the basement, with whips and chains? Shouldn't there be wicked looking torture devices and lots of leather harnesses – things like that? This room... well it looks so *ordinary!*"

"You still don't get it, do you?"

She looked at me then, her expression confused and unsure. She threw her arms wide in a gesture of helplessness. "I guess I don't," she said softly. "But I want to."

I stalked across the floor towards her, my steps light, my eyes never leaving hers. I felt my gaze smoldering and her expression changed subtly. Her eyes became wider, not with alarm but with awareness.

"It's not the room that commands obedience. It's not the props, or the décor. It's not the fear of any piece of equipment that compels a submissive to obey, and nor is it the menace of any threat. It's the man that a woman submits herself to, Leticia. Not the room.

"A good Master can be standing in a crowd or standing on a bright sunny beach. It shouldn't matter. When he speaks, it is everything he stands for and represents that induces the woman to obey him. All the fancy props, all of the intimidating atmosphere in the world can't make a good Master, and nor can it compel a woman to obedience. The man is all that matters."

"So what is the point of this room?"

"As I said – it is where my submissives are trained and punished and learn discipline. It's a working room, not some film set from a porn movie. It serves a practical purpose."

She looked around the room again, trying to see it with fresh eyes. She went to the dressing table and pulled open the top drawer. There was a ball-gag, a dildo and a pair of handcuffs. That was all. In the lower drawers were several pieces of lingerie, and a riding crop.

"What is in the chest of drawers?" she asked politely.

"Rope and a collar."

She reached into the drawer and removed the handcuffs. She set them on the dresser and the clatter of the steel was loud in the silence. She set the dildo beside the handcuffs, then pushed the drawer slowly closed. Leticia picked up the handcuffs and dangled them from the tip of one finger. She looked at me with a playful, provocative smile on her lips.

"Are these real?"

"Yes."

She inspected the handcuffs carefully. "I've always wondered..." she confessed, and her voice trailed away.

"Wondered what? Exactly?"

She shrugged. "I've always wondered how it would feel to be handcuffed," Leticia said. "The idea of being restrained like that kind of freaks me out, but it also fascinates me. Does that make sense?"

"It does."

She tugged on the cuffs to test the links. "What is the difference between being handcuffed in front of your body and behind your body? Is there a difference?"

I nodded.

"I think there is. I always cuff new submissives in front of their body when we begin their training. It just gives them a little more assurance. Once the bond of trust between us builds, then I might cuff their hands behind their backs. It depends on what aspect of training I am focusing on."

"There are different types of training for submissives?"

"Many," I said. "Sometimes the session is about discipline and control. At other times it might be about obedience, or learning submissive positions. It all depends on the person, and where I feel they need to become more competent."

Leticia's eyes drifted back down to the cuffs. "Do you have the key to these?"

"Yes," I said. "It's in the bottom drawer."

Leticia dug in the drawer and found the key. She unlocked the cuffs. "Can I try them on?"

"Do you trust me?"

"Can I hold the key?"

"Only if you don't trust me."

She thought about that. "Will you give me the key once you have handcuffed me?"

"Yes," I said. "You can hold the key once the cuffs are fastened."

I still hadn't moved. I stood near the window and watched her, enjoying the lithe way she moved and the sway of her hips.

Leticia gave me a long speculative glance and then made her decision. She held out the cuffs and the key to me. I took them from her and fastened the handcuffs around her wrists. I held the small length of steel chain and raised her arms above her head. Leticia smiled, but it was edged with sudden nervousness. I felt her tremble.

"What are you doing?"

"This," I said casually. I stepped close to her and lowered her cuffed arms over my head so they were wrapped around my neck and our bodies were pressed together. Leticia gasped.

I was standing within the circle of her arms. I smiled into her face and arched an eyebrow wickedly. I took the key to the handcuffs and held it up, close to her face.

"Open your mouth," I ordered her softly.

"What for?" Leticia's voice was wary with caution.

"So I can keep my promise," I said smoothly. "I'm giving you back the key."

Leticia's eyes flicked from my face, down to the key between my fingers, and then urgently back to my face. She opened her mouth and gave a little nervous shudder.

I gently placed the key on her bottom lip. She closed her mouth to hold the key and stop it falling to the floor.

"See how easy it is, Leticia? Do you see what a good Master might do to you?" I asked. "Now you are handcuffed, and we're standing so close together that I can feel your heart racing and see the hectic look in your eyes. I can reach out and undress you. I can unfasten every button on your blouse, and then unhook your bra. I could suck and lick your breasts until your nipples were hard, and then reach up underneath your skirt and explore the heat between your thighs. I could slide my fingers inside your panties and tease your clit until you were whimpering and weak – and there's nothing you can do, nothing you can say. If you open your mouth, the key will fall to the floor. You'll never be able to pick it up again."

My voice as I spoke was like a soft caress, but Leticia's eyes began to widen as the realization began to dawn on her and she understood at last how vulnerable she was: how exposed. Her panic was a shadow behind her eyes, flickering across her face like a little spark that threatened to catch fire and consume her.

She shifted her weight anxiously

"Will you be a good girl?" I asked softly.

Leticia nodded her head vigorously.

I smiled warmly, as if her answer pleased me. "And do you understand now that it is the man that matters, not any fancy room or intimidating props?"

Leticia nodded again. She made a sound like she was humming.

I smiled again. Then I eased myself from within the circle of her arms. Leticia put her hands to her mouth and spat the key into her palm.

I took it from her and unlocked the cuffs. I dropped them back onto the dresser, and the noise was deliberate and brutally loud. Then I turned back to Leticia.

"Now, after that simple demonstration, do you really want to continue with the dildo?"

Leticia laughed, but there was a reedy tremulous shake to the sound. "You made your point," she said and a bright flush of color spread across her cheeks. "Boy, did you make your point."

I put the dildo back into the drawer, but left the handcuffs where I had dropped them. I took a long deep breath, like I was closing one mental door and opening another.

"My father died not long after I moved back from Los Angeles," I said. "I sold the family estate and built this place. Over the next couple of years I spent time with several women – and then one day I met Caroline. She is the woman who lived with me for the past three years. She wore these handcuffs. She left six months ago."

Leticia turned back to me and studied my face carefully as though trying to read my expression. "I see," she said softly. She wasn't sure how to react.

"Do you miss her?"

"No."

"Oh. Is she still involved in your life at all?"

"No."

Leticia was standing beside the dressing table. I saw her eyes flicker towards her handbag, like she should be writing this down. She started to move, but I moved faster. I prowled towards her and stopped only when we were inches apart. I heard Leticia draw in a sudden snatch of breath and saw her body become tense. I could smell the fragrance of her. I could see the tiny throb of a pulse at her temple. Her lipstick was pink and glossy, so her lips looked full and ripe.

I touched her shoulder and felt little sparks of fire shoot back up my arm.

"Do ut des," I simmered softly. "I want you to answer me honestly. Did you go home this afternoon and pleasure yourself on your bed, with your hand tied to the headboard?"

Leticia swallowed, nervous, anxious. Her eyes searched mine, and then her gaze became dreamy like a sleepwalker. "Yes," she whispered. She closed her eyes and I saw the long thick lashes interlace. She made a soft noise in the back of her throat.

"And did you come, Leticia?"

"Yes," she breathed.

"Tell me what you fantasized about while you were laying there with your legs spread and your fingers touching yourself."

"You," she said in a sob. "I fantasized about you kissing me."

"What kind of kisses?"

"Light, soft and sexy," she whispered. "Along my throat, down to my breast, and then suddenly fiercer and more urgent ones – ones that burned my skin."

"Ones like this…?"

Leticia's eyes blinked open, misty and glistening – and I kissed her.

I took her possessively, my mouth forcing hers open so that her soft pink lips parted like flowering petals. I felt her respond. She shuddered voluptuously and there was a deep yearning moan in the back of her throat. I felt her arms wrap around my neck and her body flattened hard against my chest so that I could feel the firm resilience of her breasts beneath the sheer fabric of her top. I felt her fingers entwine themselves in the hair at the nape of my neck, and I slid one hand around the narrowness of her waist as she arched her back and pushed forward with her hips.

I heard her gasp as she felt the hardness of me, and the heat between our bodies seemed to melt us together. I slid my tongue within her mouth and she hunted it hungrily with her own. I inhaled the scent of her, dominated her with my lips so that she bowed back from the intensity, like a tree before a rising wind.

I could hear my blood sizzle in my veins, and I could feel the wild thump of my heart. I tightened my grip around her waist and with my other hand I cupped the side of her face, marveling in the soft smoothness of her skin.

We broke apart for a split second – just long enough for Leticia to draw a single trembling breath – and then I kissed her again until I heard her sob weakly, as though she were drowning.

I leaned back. Leticia's eyelids fluttered like the beating wings of a butterfly. Her lips parted slightly in a silent gasp.

"You took my breath away..." she marveled softly. One hand drifted to her mouth. She touched her kiss-enflamed lips with the tip of a finger as if the taste of me was still upon her, and her lip trembled, still wet and glistening.

I stared down into Leticia's face and the wild urgency within me faded and turned suddenly to a cold uncoiling dread. There was agony in my expression as my arm went heavy around her waist and dropped to my side.

I took a sudden step back.

Leticia's eyes were desperate and bewildered.

"Jonah...?"

I took another step back. Suddenly the room was small and claustrophobic. I felt a thudding ache of remorse and saw the shadowy reflection of my face in the dressing table mirror. There were dark guilty smudges, like bruises, beneath my eyes that I hadn't noticed before.

Leticia took an urgent pace towards me. I held up my hands and she went still. "No," I said. "I made a mistake."

"Mistake?" Leticia shook her head in disbelief so that her hair shimmered and swished. "No, Jonah. You didn't. I'm glad you kissed me. I've been wanting you to do that for days."

I felt the cold seep through my body until my veins turned to ice. "You don't understand," I said and my voice sounded hollow and empty in my own ears. "I shouldn't have kissed you, Leticia. I brought you here to write my story – *not to make you part of it.*"

Leticia looked close to tears. Her eyes misted. "But I wanted it!"

I shook my head dismissively. "You don't know what you want. You think you want this lifestyle – and maybe you do," I said, my tone remote. "But you don't want me. Believe me. I'm not the man you want in your life."

She reached a hand out towards me. It fluttered in the air and then fell back to her side like a wounded bird. Her face was filled with anguish and sudden despair. Leticia was shaking her head slowly from side to side. Her eyes brimmed with tears, making them seem huge and glistening. She sobbed in a sharp breath, and a single teardrop spilled down her cheek.

I looked away. I felt the shutters lower over my eyes and my gaze became distant.

Bastard.

I thrust my hands into my pockets as though to restrain myself.

Leticia's mouth twisted in distress. "Jonah – please," she pleaded. "Please talk to me. Tell me what I did wrong. Did I not kiss you well enough? I'm sorry! I'm not very experienced... and I've never been with a man like you. If you give me another chance..."

I shook my head. She wrung her hands and I felt her trying to reach out to me. "Did you want more? I can give it to you, Jonah. Just give me some time to –"

I backed towards the door. I held it open. "I think you should go," I said coldly. "If not for your sake, then please, do it for me."

* * *

It rained the next day. Dark sullen clouds swept in from the west and blanketed the mountains so that the sky was grey and cold and bleak. Rain swept across the ranges in grey misting curtains, and the driveway filled with puddles as downpours burst upon the roof and echoed through the empty rooms.

I sat in the study. The drapes were drawn. Flames leaped from the fireplace flickering and crackling with light and sparks, but still I was cold. It was a cold that no warmth could reach – a cold deep in my bones.

I sat in the study, sifting through documents and paperwork that had accumulated on my desk, picking at them the way a man with no appetite picks at food.

I heard the phone ring downstairs, echoed an instant later through the extension phone on the side-table next to the big leather chair. I looked at the phone, listened to it ring – waited for it to stop, suddenly frozen as though the slightest move might somehow reveal me.

When the work was done, I went to the fireplace and threw another log onto the flames. It burst in a flare of sparks, and I drew myself to my feet like a weary old man and began to slowly pace the room.

The phone rang again an hour later. I stood in the shadows and watched it until the sound was cut off abruptly, and I was left alone in the silence.

The specter of Trigg's warnings hung over me like a gloomy pall, seeming like a burden I had failed to carry. She knew me so well. She knew me like no other woman ever had; my fears, my frailties. And yet she didn't really know me at all.

Not Jonah Noble, the man.

The phone rang again and my hand reached for it, hanging in the air an inch above the receiver so that I could almost feel the urgent vibration of it. I hesitated.

Then I picked the phone up.

"Jonah?"

It was Leticia, but then I always knew it would be. I felt the sound of her voice pierce like a blade.

"Yes."

"Jonah, it's me, Leticia. Please don't hang up!"

I stayed silently on the line. I could hear the ragged sound of her breathing loud and anguished in my ear.

"I wanted to apologize to you," she said softly, and I could tell by the broken little crack in her voice that she had been weeping. "I'm sorry about what happened yesterday. I... I was very unprofessional. I want you to give me another chance to finish the interview we started. I want to finish writing your story."

I stared vacantly into the fire, seeing nothing but flickering light for a very long time. And then the sound of her words cut through the numbed haze and my eyes came slowly back into focus. "I want that too," I said.

* * *

It was still raining hard when Leticia arrived that evening.

She parked in front of the house. I watched the car pull up in a splash of brown muddy water and the headlights go dark. I saw the driver's door swing open, and Leticia made a sudden rush for the front door. She came gasping and squealing into the foyer, and stood dripping water onto the tiles while she shrugged off her coat and combed her fingers through her hair.

She looked like a half-drowned kitten.

Leticia held out her hand to me like we were perfect strangers. "Thank you for seeing me again, Mr. Noble."

I shook her hand stiffly. It was wet and cold. She shivered involuntarily and I led her up the winding staircase and into the study.

The room was warm – the fire still burned. I led Leticia over to the fireplace and she stood before the flames with her back to me for long moments as tiny tendrils of steam began to lift from her clothes.

She was wearing a simple white sweater and comfortable jeans. Her shoes were wet. She slipped her feet out of them and nudged them closer to the fire, then turned, barefoot and wet, and smiled at me bravely.

"You didn't have to come tonight," I said. "This could have waited."

She shook her head. "No, it couldn't. I needed to see you. I needed to apologize for what happened. It was my fault. I should have been more professional."

I shook my head and sighed. "It wasn't your fault, Leticia. We both know that. I made the mistake, and I regret it. My hope now is that we can forget what happened – set the whole incident aside – and continue on with the interview. Deal?"

She nodded. "Deal," she agreed.

I went down the hallway to my bedroom and came back into the study holding one of my shirts. I handed it to Leticia.

"Take the sweater off and put this on."

She accepted the shirt. She draped it over the back of the sofa and began to peel off her sodden top. I turned my back and heard the rustle of fabric.

I walked a slow circuit of the room, halting to elaborately study the brushstrokes of a painting, picking up a book from the side-table and replacing it on a shelf. Finally I paused and turned back to face the room.

Leticia had changed into the shirt. She had rolled up the sleeves almost to the point of her elbows, and buttoned it all the way up to the collar. It swamped her body, and still she looked good.

She stretched out the wet sweater before the fire to dry and then sat down on the edge of the sofa. It was dark in the room. I paced in the shadows, and Leticia's eyes followed me, her face painted golden by the flickering firelight. She reached down to her bag to fetch her notebook.

"You told me that you had a live-in submissive for the last three years," she began delicately, her voice brittle. "Could you tell me more?"

I nodded. "Her name was Caroline," I said.

Silence.

"Can you tell me about her?"

"Caroline was a woman who initially applied for the job as my secretary." I said. I heard my own words sounding stilted and forced. "I have a secretary who works from a downtown office, and one day a week she comes here to the house so I can dictate letters and attend to business. She brings the correspondence to me and we deal with it all on one day. That was the job Caroline had applied for."

"So she was your secretary initially?"

"No," I said. "She applied for the position. Frankly, she wasn't suitable. There were better applicants." There was a hollow distant tone to my voice.

Leticia wrote a brief note and then looked back up at me. Her legs were crossed. Absently, I noticed her toenails were painted bright red.

"So how did she become your submissive?" Leticia asked with patient politeness.

I shrugged. "A week later I saw her at a gathering."

"A BDSM gathering?"

"No. Not officially. It was a party at a friend's home. A lot of those friends were involved or interested in the lifestyle."

"Do you attend BDSM functions, or visit BDSM clubs?"

"No," I shook my head. "I like the lifestyle. It suits me, but I've never been part of the scene socially. BDSM clubs never made a lot of sense to me. I always saw it as like having too many roosters together in the same hen-house. Every man who considers himself a dom just tries to out alpha-male everyone else. It becomes a pissing competition."

Leticia bowed her head over her notebook and jotted another note. Her hair was still wet, and it was curling down around her ears in random swirling tendrils.

"So have you always been private about your lifestyle?"

"Yes. Up until the moment I began this interview with you."

Leticia flipped back a couple of pages into her notebook and then looked up thoughtfully through the tense strain. "So you saw Caroline at a party with a group of friends who were in the lifestyle."

"Yes. I've already told you that."

Leticia looked up sharply and I saw a flicker of anguish drift across her eyes. She took a breath and pressed on.

"So what happened between you and Caroline at the party?"

I started to pace, but somehow I just seemed to run out of steam. I stood, like I was suddenly broken, in the middle of the floor for a moment. I tried again. I got as far as the door, but I could feel my anger and frustration rising. I felt a burning lump in my throat – and then impulse took over.

I turned on Leticia and she must have sensed the tension in my body. "This isn't working," I clenched my jaw.

Leticia lowered her head, tucked the notebook into her bag and stood meekly. "You want me to go again, don't you."

I crossed the room in three strides. Leticia's eyes became enormous with uncertainty. She stood, frozen, anxious as I hunted towards her.

I took her arm and she stood rigid. I leaned towards her. Her arms hung by her sides like those of a rag doll. I drew her closer to me and she was unresisting. "No," I said. "I don't want you to leave, dammit. I want you back. I want what we had back. I want to talk to you like I did before – not like this. Not like there is something between us."

She stared at me, huge startled eyes in her young innocent face. She looked like she might suffocate. I felt her trembling.

"Let's get this straight," I said. "Let me explain what happened when I kissed you – and what happened afterwards."

Leticia didn't say anything. She nodded her head and waited.

I stepped away, paced the room, hands thrust deep into my pockets, my head bowed, like a shark circling prey.

For a long time the only sound was the echo of my footsteps as I assembled the words in my head.

I'm an impulsive man. I don't think everything to death before I say or do something. That doesn't mean I'm not thoughtful and deliberate – it just means that I always speak my mind. It's how I get to sleep at night.

Only one thing needed to remain unsaid...

I took a deep breath, and the words spilled out – words from the heart – the raw truth, delivered in Jonah Noble style.

"I want you to know this – because it's the truth. When I kissed you, I didn't want to stop. I wanted to keep kissing you. I backed away to protect you – not because of anything you did wrong. I wanted to keep you safe from me."

I looked to Leticia. She opened her mouth to say something, but I shook my head curtly and she sat back down on the sofa. "I need you to write my story. Hell, I need you in my life. I like the way you smile. I like your sweet beautiful innocence. And I want you around me. I feel happy when we're together. But I'll never love you, Leticia," I shook my head sorrowfully. "I'll never love you."

Leticia looked pale and timid. Her eyes were fixed on mine, following my every move.

"I've never loved any woman," I said. "I've cared for them, protected them, been a Master to them, and lusted after them – but not once have I allowed myself to fall in love. And maybe I never will. I can accept that – but I know you can't. I know you – maybe better than you know yourself. You're young, and you can do better than to give your heart to someone like me who will never love you back. I want you – and I need you, but I don't want you to fall in love with me."

"What makes you so sure that I will?"

I smiled, but there was no humor. "Because I'm fighting with all my strength to stop falling in love with you."

Leticia cleared her throat. "Maybe with time..."

I shook my head again. "We can talk all night, but it's not going to change the way I need this relationship to be. It can't be sexual, because, for a woman, with sex comes emotion. It cannot be a BDSM relationship, because you don't even know what you want from life yet, and I don't want to be responsible for your safety and welfare. And it can't be love, Leticia, because I can't handle that."

"Then what – what do you want from me, Jonah? Do you just want me to write your story and have you look at me with dead vacant eyes like I'm just some kind of associate that you know for a few weeks and then forget?"

"I want your friendship," I said. "It's all I am asking for. Anything more is unsafe for you – if it becomes more than that it will end in tears and heartbreak, and I don't want to hurt you any more than I already have."

Leticia sat silently for a long time, her gaze far away and remote. She looked lost and alone and tragic. Finally she nodded. "Okay, Jonah," she said softly. "If the only way it can be between us is the way that it was, then we'll make it that way again."

I stared at her, and figured that she could not have possibly found a more complicated way of expressing a simple answer.

* * *

I led Leticia downstairs and into the kitchen. I felt we needed a change of environment in order to change the mood. She sat at the kitchen table while I scalded myself with hot water making coffee for us.

I carried the mugs to the table and deliberately sat at the chair beside her.

She turned so that we were facing each other, close in the soft light of a lamp. She sipped her coffee, made an excruciating face, and then smiled weakly.

She set the mug down on the table and pushed it away from her like maybe it was poison.

"You told me in the study that we couldn't have just a sexual relationship because – for women – sex comes with emotion. Can you explain that?"

I didn't drink the coffee.

"I can," I said. "The problem with most relationships is a lack of understanding. You see, women need to feel loved in order to want sex. And men need sex, in order to feel loved."

Leticia played the words back in her mind, and then nodded with slow dawning appreciation. "That's very profound," she said.

I nodded. "They're not my words. Someone much smarter and wiser than me came up with that, but I think it sums up the problem between the sexes perfectly."

Leticia nodded. "You're a smooth talker, Jonah," she said. "Your voice, your words. In fact you're very smooth at everything you do."

Suddenly the suggestion of sexuality in her comment occurred to her, and Leticia fell guiltily silent. She looked down at her handbag and then across at the coffee cup, as if she couldn't meet my eyes.

"I didn't mean it to sound the way it did," she apologized softly.

I arched my eyebrow in a roguish gesture of innocence. "I don't know what you're talking about," I said, and brushed the awkwardness away. Leticia smiled into my face and nodded. She relaxed again.

"Caroline," she began. "I'd like to know more about her, and how you met. I'd like to know about that night at the party. Will you tell me, please?"

It felt better between us then. The ice had thawed enough so that the memories came freely back to me and I began to talk.

"Caroline was beautiful," I said simply. "She had classic features: high cheekbones, and exotic slanted eyes. She looked like a modern-day Cleopatra, with long straight black hair and a figure like a delicate vase that curved and flared in perfect proportions. She was quite tall, and moved with a feline grace. She was simply stunning."

"How old was she?"

"We were the same age," I said.

Leticia made a face, frowned, and then wrote something into her notebook. Then she scratched it out and wrote something else.

"And the party?" she looked up at me. "Tell me what happened. How did you and Caroline become Master and submissive?"

I sat back in the chair and stared at the far wall. I could see Leticia's face from the corner of my eye, watching me with some kind of intent fascination. I went back through my memories to the first night I had seen Caroline in a social situation.

"We exchanged small-talk," I said. "But she didn't seem surprised to see me at that party. It was only much later that I found out she had talked herself into an invitation, as part of a deliberate plan for us to meet again."

Leticia's voice seemed to come from out of the shadows. "She must have been very desperate to meet you."

I didn't answer. I saw Caroline in my mind's eye. I remembered the sights and sounds of that evening. I remembered the cool breeze blowing across the beachside house, and watching Caroline disappear into the fringe of trees that bordered the property. I had followed her down onto the sand, and she stood there in the moonlight waiting for me.

"We ended up on a beach," I told Leticia at last. "The breeze was coming off the ocean, and it flattened the flimsy dress Caroline was wearing against her body so that she might have been naked. The fabric wrapped around her hips, and tugged firm around the jut of her breasts. I stood back and admired her, because she was truly a thing of beauty.

"'I didn't know you knew these people,' I said to her. 'I didn't know you were into the BDSM lifestyle'. She smiled at me – it was one of those sexy, seductive smiles that only a woman knows how to deliver – and then she told me that she hadn't known when she arrived for the interview that I was looking for a submissive, as well as a secretary.

"She kicked off her sandals and strolled down to the water's edge. I stood on the beach and watched her. The moon was rising, and the sky was full of stars. Caroline glanced over her shoulder at me and then looked back at the ocean. She slipped her dress from her shoulders and let it fall to the sand. She was completely naked underneath. She stood staring at the waves for a long moment, and then turned back to face me. Her legs were long, her skin the color of caramel, and her breasts were full.

"She cupped her hands beneath her breasts and squeezed her nipples between her fingers. She looked up at me with hooded eyes, and there was an invitation in her expression, as clear as if she had spoken the words aloud.

"I went to her, and we stood in the wet sand. I circled her like I was inspecting some exquisite treasure and she stood obediently still. I could hear her breathing as I came up behind her. I told her to get on her knees. She made a small, hissing sound of arousal as though her breath had hitched in her throat. She lowered herself to her knees and bowed her head submissively.

"It was like some ancient ritual – some kind of ceremony of possession."

I stopped speaking suddenly.

Did I just say that? The description sounded ridiculous, but I couldn't find a better way to explain how it had felt that night on the beach. I looked across at Leticia, expecting to see her smiling at me like I was a fool. She wasn't. She was staring at my mouth, and her lips were slightly parted, glistening and full.

"I stood before Caroline and put my finger under her chin. She lifted her face to mine and stared passively up at me.

"'If you want to submit to me you should know that I expect your unquestioning obedience,' I told her. She said she expected nothing less. She told me she was willing to give herself to me and learn to please me. I told her to stand and follow me back to the fringe of trees.

"Did she?" Leticia asked.

I nodded. "I led her naked to a tree and she put her back against the trunk. I told her to spread her legs, and she shuffled her feet wide apart. Her breathing became erratic. She had her hands by her side. I told her to put them on her head and lace her fingers together. Her eyes were wide, and there was a recklessness in her expression, like this was the realization of some secret thrill for her. I ran my fingers down between her breasts and then drew them lazily up again so they circled around one nipple.

"Caroline began to squirm. Her hips rocked, and then she tilted her pelvis forward. Her nipple hardened and I slowly lowered my lips and sucked it into my mouth.

"I heard Caroline groan, and then felt her hand on my shoulder as though to hold me to her breast. I broke contact and my eyes flashed. I told her to put her hands back on her head, and if she moved them again I would take her dress and leave her naked on the beach. She groaned again, but the sound was more like a stifled plea. She did as I told her, and I sucked her nipple back between my lips, and then ran my hand slowly down towards her parted thighs… and then stopped."

Leticia looked up in complete surprise. "Stopped?"

"Yes," I said.

"So… you didn't um… touch her…?"

I looked at Leticia like she was insane. "Of course not," I said. "Not immediately. That would have been a mistake."

She shook her head and I saw the same insane look I had given her, reflected. She didn't understand.

"I don't understand," she said.

I scraped the chair back and got to my feet. Leticia knew what was coming. She saw me begin to pace, and she immediately flipped over to a new blank page and flexed her cramping fingers in expectation.

"Leticia, one of a Master's most potent, powerful weapons is…" I left the sentence unfinished, but continued to pace the floor. After a minute, Leticia made a sound like a subtle cough to get my attention.

"Is what?" she asked, frowning with curiosity. "What's the potent weapon?"

I smiled. "Anticipation."

"That's a weapon?"

I nodded. "Anticipation is more potent than a whip and more compelling than handcuffs. The ability to tease and arouse a woman is a subtle skill few men ever bother to learn," I said. "But learning the art of anticipation can make a woman go weak at the knees with longing."

"I'm listening..." Leticia said. "But I don't follow."

"I'll give you an example," I smiled mischievously. "Come over here."

Leticia rose from her chair obediently and stood facing me.

"Now close your eyes."

"Why?"

"Because I'm going to touch your shoulder, and then your cheek."

She looked puzzled. She shrugged and closed her eyes. Then I touched her shoulder gently and slid my hand across the soft skin of her cheek. She opened her eyes again.

"How was that?" I asked.

She shrugged. "Um...okay."

I nodded. "Because you knew exactly what to expect. Now close your eyes again, and keep them closed."

When Leticia closed her eyes, I waited for a long moment, until she began to move her head as though listening to some soft secret sound. "Jonah...?"

I reached out and brushed my hand down the soft trembling skin of her throat and she let out an involuntary gasp. I withdrew my hand, and waited, counting out the long seconds. Leticia smiled a little nervously, and then I traced my fingertip down her forearm. She shuddered, and her breath caught in her throat. She opened her eyes, her face lightly flushed.

"Anticipating is expectation," I said. "It's the mystery of not knowing, and the heightening of all a woman's senses. Anticipation draws out the moment so that the moment then becomes exquisite," I explained. "And it is only something as powerful as anticipation that can elevate an ordinary touch to a breathtaking caress."

Leticia sat back in her chair as though I had just revealed some profound mystery of the universe, while I continued re-telling my first encounter with Caroline.

"Caroline held her breath for as long as my hand remained unmoving, and then, as I edged it slowly lower, she let out a gasp. Her sex was shaved smooth, and my fingers slipped over the velvety soft lips of her pussy.

"'You sought me out tonight,' I said in a whisper. My mouth was just an inch from her ear. Her eyes were closed. 'Why?'

"Caroline licked her lips. I kept my fingers teasing the flesh of her pussy and used the wetness of her to gently massage her clit. She bunched her hands into tight little fists of restraint.

"'I want you as my Master,' she told me. She said she had been involved in the lifestyle for over a year but had left her previous Master. When I asked her why, she said he hadn't been man enough to dominate her.

"I asked Caroline what made her so sure I would be interested in a woman like her – and then I slid two of my fingers inside her. She arched her back so that her hips and breasts strained forward, her body bowed and trembling. Her mouth fell open in a soft purr of arousal as I played the tips of my fingers around her sex.

"She pleaded for me to take her on as my submissive. She promised she would deny me nothing. I told her it all depended on the taste of her pussy – and then I eased my fingers from inside her and held them up close to my face.

"Caroline's eyes fluttered open. My fingers were slick and glistening with the juices of her arousal. I slowly licked at the taste, and then slid my fingers into my mouth.

"I narrowed my eyes, kept my expression stern and made her wait.

"You taste like honey," I told her.

Leticia was fascinated. She had moved as I spoke. Now she was sitting on the edge of her chair, with her elbows on her knees and her hands cupping her chin. "Did she? I mean, did she really taste like that?"

I gave Leticia my serious face. "Leticia, no woman tastes like honey – but every man should tell the woman he is with that she does."

"What does that mean?"

"It means that every woman I have ever known intimately has been inhibited and self-conscious about the way their pussy might taste to a man."

"Why?"

I shrugged. "How the hell would I know? You tell me. All I know is that women relax and let themselves go sexually once a man reassures her that he loves the way she tastes. I tell women they taste like honey. That's the line I use, because I want them to relax and I want them to enjoy the experience of my tongue deep between their legs and licking their clit. Good sex isn't possible if the woman I'm with is tense and anxious."

"Is that in the Jonah Noble big book of rules?"

"Yes," I said. "Page two."

I finally screwed up my courage and sipped the coffee. It tasted like drain cleaner. Somehow I had mixed powdered coffee, milk, sugar and hot water, and created something that was probably toxic. I took the cups to the sink and found a bottle of whisky in a cupboard.

"So what happened with Caroline, after..."

"After what?"

"After... you know... your fingers..."

"No. I don't know what you mean," I said. "Say it."

Leticia looked at me like I was a brute, and her lips compressed into a thin frosty line. "What happened after you licked Caroline's pussy juices off your fingers and told her she tasted like honey?" she asked, holding my gaze defiantly, but blushing like a schoolgirl as she did.

I nodded, satisfied.

"I put my hand back between her spread legs and rubbed her gently until her hips were rocking with the pace of my fingers. And as I touched and teased her, I spoke quietly into her ear.

"I told her she was to come to my house the following evening. I told her she was to wear lingerie. I told her she shouldn't make plans to go home until the following morning. Caroline nodded obediently – but by that point if I had told her to steal the Crown Jewels she probably would have agreed. I had her on the edge of her orgasm and deliberately held her there, right on the brink of exploding, but never quite touching her firmly enough to spark her release. Her teeth were bared, her lips pared back like she might snarl, and she sucked in short ragged breaths with growing desperation.

"When I was satisfied that Caroline had heard all of my instructions, and when I was sure she would obey, I left her and strolled back to the party."

"You left her? You didn't let her orgasm?"

"No."

"That was mean!"

"It kept her keen," I countered. "It told her, without me saying a word, that I had control, and that I made the decisions."

"Did she come to your house the next night?" Leticia prompted.

"Yes."

"And did she stay the night?"

"Yes. In my bed."

"And so you took her as your submissive and she lived with you, right?"

"Not immediately, no. But over the course of a few weeks we grew to understand each other. She was smart, sexy, independent and strong willed. I liked those qualities in her," I explained. "Finally I told her to gather her things from her apartment and to live with me."

"As your submissive?"
"Yes. As my submissive."
Leticia chewed her bottom lip as she made notes. I waited in the silence until she looked up at me again. "Did you sign contracts?"
I blinked. Leticia's expression was intense and earnest.
She was serious.
"No," I laughed. "What made you ask a question like that?"
Leticia shrugged and seemed to shrink in the chair. "I... I thought submissives signed contracts," she said meekly. "I thought it was like an agreement – those limits you asked me about. I thought contracts were signed so that everything was spelled out before the training started."
I shook my head dismissively. "Leticia, what would be the point of a contract – really? Think about it for a moment. If you were my submissive and I wrote down all the things I expected from you, and you agreed with that list – we wouldn't need a contract, would we?"
"No..."
"Remember I told you everything in BDSM must be safe, sane and consensual?"
"Yes..."
"Well if you signed a contract including an agreement that you would kneel before me and suck my cock six times a day – for example – suppose you changed your mind one day, *and withdrew your consent.* What would be the point of the contract? If I enforce the agreement, you

would do so unwillingly – which goes against the golden rules of the lifestyle."

"So you don't ever have a contract agreement?"

"No," I said. "But I would happily sign one if it gave a sense of reassurance to a submissive. I could understand the idea on that basis. If a submissive was interested in serving me, and she asked me to sign a contract that in some way gave her comfort about her safety and her care, and her right to leave the relationship at any stage she wanted, then I would happily sign."

There was a brief moment of silence and then I stabbed a finger into the air suddenly, like Sherlock Holmes about to reveal the name of a culprit in a murder mystery book. "But... that doesn't mean I don't have rules," I said. "And I make those rules perfectly clear from the beginning. The rules spell out what behaviors I require and what attitude I expect. If a submissive fails to meet my expectations, they are dismissed. If a submissive – at any stage – no longer wants to adhere to those rules, they are free to leave, no questions asked. That's the way I do things, because that's the way it works for me. Other Masters might do things differently."

Leticia looked suddenly enthusiastic. "Can you tell me some of the rules?"

"No." I said. "To see the rules, you would need a copy of the Jonah Noble big book of rules." And then I smiled because I wasn't totally convinced Leticia realized I was joking.

"The rules vary from submissive to submissive," I said. "It depends on each woman's needs, their particular interests within the lifestyle, and the behaviors I feel they should improve in order to become better at submitting and serving. It also depends on their fetishes. I don't have a generic list, and just change the person's name at the top of the page. It's a lot more personal than that."

Leticia spent a long time making more notes, faithfully recording everything I said. "Was Caroline a good submissive?"

I considered that question. "In some ways yes, and in others she required a lot of training," I said.

"Was she a good submissive sexually?"

"Yes. Absolutely."

Leticia frowned. "What made her good in... in the bedroom?"

"The same thing that makes every woman good in the bedroom," I shrugged, "her enthusiasm."

Leticia was paying close attention. "Care to explain?"

I walked slowly around the kitchen. I had the glass of whisky in one hand and I stuffed my other hand into my pocket. "I think if you gave most men the choice between a highly skilled woman in the bedroom, and a woman who was insatiable, they would choose the insatiable one more often than not," I said. "I certainly always have." I swallowed the last of the whisky and set the glass down on the edge of the table, but I didn't stop walking. "A gorgeous woman who wants sex once a month is a lot less desirable to a man than an average-looking woman who wants sex every night. Caroline was gorgeous, and insatiable."

Leticia looked at me, disbelieving. "You're trying to tell me that it doesn't matter to a man how good a woman is in bed, the only thing that really matters is whether she is an enthusiastic lover?"

"Yes," I said. "For most men, their sex life is measured in quantity, not quality."

Leticia looked up from her notebook, her expression confused. "I need to go back to Caroline," she changed tack. She seemed extremely curious about Caroline – much more so than she had been about Claire or Sherry from my distant past. "You told me you lived with her for three years?"

"Yes. She left six months ago."

"And you *never* loved the woman?"

"No." I said. I could see by the look on Leticia's face that she didn't believe me, and I drew a deep breath and began to pace in circles around the kitchen.

"You need to understand the origins of the relationship, Leticia. When Caroline came to me it was as my submissive. We never courted, there was no romance, and we never fell in love, because it was not the objective or purpose of the relationship.

"Falling in love with your submissive is about the biggest mistake a Master can make," I told her. "As soon as you start to see the woman kneeling before you with 'loving eyes' you begin to moderate everything. Suddenly hard and fast rules are no longer quite as rigid, and all the aspects of discipline and obedience that are the bedrock of a BDSM relationship begin to disintegrate. It is far easier to start a relationship built around the BDSM lifestyle than it is to turn a loving relationship into one.

"It's been my experience that BDSM play only really has the chance to work when the man can look at a woman with 'hard eyes'."

"Hard eyes?" Leticia repeated. "As opposed to 'loving eyes'?"

"Exactly," I said. "'Hard eyes' is that detached, slightly remote attitude, where the man's emotional attachment to the woman is suspended, or pushed into the background temporarily – just far enough into the background so he can give the woman the experience she craves without him feeling restrained by any emotional or romantic considerations."

I paused for a moment, playing those last comments back in my head. "I'm talking about committed couples here. I don't mean the man needs to see the woman as an object, or have no feelings for her at all – I simply mean that the man has to kind of 'step back' from the normal feelings he might have for the woman, temporarily. He can't be blinded to the woman's feelings or needs, or safety – just slightly detached."

Leticia frowned. "It doesn't sound easy."

"For a lot of men it's not," I agreed. "Right now, guys in loving relationships with their wives all around America are suddenly being asked to spank, whip or maybe handcuff their woman. Most men in a relationship confronted in that way would say something like *'I don't want to hurt you'* – and despite all of the wife's reassurances, the guy won't budge, because he has always seen the woman through 'loving eyes'. It's hard for him to switch, and discover that place where he can become detached just sufficiently enough to make BDSM work without guilt, or inhibition."

Leticia was still frowning. Maybe I wasn't doing a very good job of explaining myself.

"If a couple first formed a loving relationship, the guy often has trouble suddenly seeing the woman with 'hard eyes'. It is something that takes a lot of patient encouragement from the woman to alter the situation. Does this make any sense?"

Leticia didn't answer for a full minute after she had finished writing down everything I had said. She put her pen down with a sigh and swept hair away from her eyes.

"I don't think your explanation is going to end up as an encyclopedia definition. But yeah, it makes sense."

"What I'm saying is that sometimes women don't understand where their husband is coming from, and why he might seem reluctant – especially with the more physical aspects of BDSM – to give some of the things she wants to experience a try. Now, maybe this couple we are talking about have been married for fifteen years and all the passion has gone from their marriage. Maybe that's why the wife wants to introduce BDSM – to put some spice into the relationship. You would think my 'loving eyes' theory would no longer hold true after a couple has been together for so long, but it doesn't really change, even though the way the couple love each other may have altered over the years. The fact is they were in love before BDSM came along and that's the obstacle the woman needs to address with small patient steps and plenty of persistence."

"Is that another secret a person browsing through Jonah Noble's big book of rules would come across?"

"Yes. There is an edited version of everything I just said on page seven." I smiled and Leticia smiled with me. I felt like we were finally back on the same wavelength, and at the same place in our relationship as we had been before I had made the mistake of kissing her.

I resumed pacing again, but for no good reason. I didn't have anything else worth saying right then. I glanced down at Leticia's notebook and saw line after line of sloping squiggles seeming to run up the page.

"You know there was a time where journalists learned shorthand for these kind of interviews," I said dryly.

Leticia nodded. "Some of the journalists at the paper like to use a Dictaphone," she said. "Or record interviews directly to their cell phone."

"But not you?"

She shook her head. "I like to have everything down on paper and everything organized," she said.

"Can you read that scrawl you have written? You must have a dozen notebooks by now filled with everything I have told you."

"Eight, actually," Leticia said. "And yes I can read it all… usually."

I went back to the kitchen counter and splashed more whisky into the bottom of my glass. I held the bottle up in silent invitation to Leticia. She hesitated with a small look of regret, then shook her head, like she really did want a drink but was denying herself. I sipped at the whisky and enjoyed the silence. The night outside was very still.

Leticia shifted her weight discreetly in the chair as if she was afraid to disturb me, and then she softly cleared her throat. My eyes came back into focus, my thoughts returned to the here-and-now.

"Do you have many memorable experiences with Caroline that you can recall – for the story?" Leticia asked.

I stood a little straighter and nodded. "The first incident that comes to mind was on a business trip," I said. "It was just a one-day meeting and an overnight stay in a hotel. I took Caroline with me."

"Not your secretary?"

I shook my head. "It was more pleasure than business," I smiled thinly. "Caroline and I were booked into one of the luxury suites on the first floor. The rooms were built around a swimming pool. I attended the meeting and left Caroline to her own devices for a few hours. When I came back to the room, I discovered that she was down by the pool. Several of the wives of my associates had gathered together to pass the afternoon."

"Did everyone else know that Caroline was your submissive?"

"No," I said. "As I have mentioned before, I'm a private man. What I do in my personal life is my business. I never mixed private affairs with those connected to my work. The people at the hotel that weekend had no idea Caroline was anything other than a beautiful companion I had brought along for company."

"Were you jealous, Jonah?" Leticia asked. "If Caroline was as beautiful as you describe her, then surely there must have been plenty of other men at the hotel – even some of your business friends – who would have been admiring her."

"I was never jealous, and never possessive," I said. "And that wasn't because I was arrogant, or because I thought I was the only good-looking man in the world. It was because I was confident that I was the only man who could give a woman like Caroline what she needed to feel fulfilled."

"Has that been your attitude with every woman you have been intimate with?"

"Of course," I said simply, and then realized the answer wasn't that simple after all. "Leticia, this is a world where free will reins, as it should. That means I believe every woman has the right to make her own choices and her own decisions about her life. She can decide to serve me as a submissive, or she can decide to leave me for another man, or another lifestyle at any time. I can't – and I would never try – to hold a woman to me who didn't want to be at my side. Ultimately, there is no point wasting energy on emotions like jealousy or being possessive. You can't keep someone from following their heart."

We had detoured off topic again. I stared down into my glass, and regrettably decided I had probably drunk enough. I left the glass on the kitchen counter.

"Where was I?"

Leticia glanced at her notebook. "Caroline was down by the pool with a group of other women. You had just finished your meeting."

I nodded.

"The suite had a wide glass sliding door that opened onto a balcony. There was some outdoor furniture in one corner, and the balcony railing was a waist-high brick wall that stretched the full width of the room. I glanced over the rail and saw Caroline. She was wearing a tiny blue bikini, and she was stretched out on a sun lounge. She saw me and lifted her sunglasses from her eyes, gave me a wave. I waved back to her, summoning her to the room.

"Caroline was in the doorway just a minute or two later. She stood barefoot on the carpet with a towel wrapped like a sarong around her waist. Her skin was shiny with perspiration and suntan lotion. She smelled of coconuts, and, after just an hour in the sun, her body had turned a healthy glowing shade of brown. I devoured her with my eyes, and she stood silently, enjoying the appreciation.

"Caroline was an exhibitionist," I explained to Leticia. "That was her particular little fetish."

Leticia wrote more notes and then sat silently flexing the cramp from her fingers while she watched me to see if I would continue. I did.

"I told Caroline to remove the towel. She touched at her waist and it fell down around her ankles. Her bikini bottoms were little more than a tiny patch of fabric, tied at each hip with pieces of string. The bikini top was no better. I could see the press of her nipples through the thin fabric, and as I watched they actually seemed to harden and enlarge before my gaze. Caroline lowered her eyes demurely. She was smiling softly to herself, playing the part of the modest submissive, yet in reality I knew she was reveling in my hungry gaze, and proud of her body and the way it affected me. She thought it gave her a silent, subtle power – and I let her think that it did."

"But it didn't? You weren't, like, obsessed with her beauty?" Leticia asked.

"No," I said. I made a sweeping gesture with my hands. "Leticia there are millions of beautiful women in the world. They're beautiful in different ways. Caroline wasn't the only attractive woman I had ever seen. In your own way, your body is every bit as beautiful as hers."

Oompf!

That was the sound of me jamming my foot into my mouth. The silence drew out into long awkward moments. Leticia said nothing. She stared fixedly down at her notebook, not daring even to glance up at me. I picked up the thread of the story and continued as if nothing had happened.

But it had.

"I told Caroline to remove her bikini bottoms," I went on. "She lifted her face to mine and we locked eyes. She tugged at a string and the fabric fell away from the soft shaved cleft of her pussy. She took a sudden short breath, and then another one.

"She reached behind her to unfasten the strings of her top but I stopped her. 'No,' I said. 'That won't be necessary'.

"She looked at me quizzically. I told her she was to go out to the balcony and lean on the brick wall. She stared at me in silence, and in the background I could still hear the voices of the other women coming from down around the pool. I asked if Mrs. Solomon was one of the women at the pool. Caroline said she was.

"Mrs. Solomon was a big woman, with a loud voice. Her husband and I had worked on a couple of real estate deals together the year before. I told Caroline to lean on the balcony wall and talk to Mrs. Solomon about her children – and to keep the conversation going, no matter what.

"Caroline didn't ask questions – although I could see confusion in her eyes and on her face. She walked out through the sliding glass doors and into the afternoon sunshine. I stood and watched her. I saw her lean on the wall – it came to the height of her navel. She stood on tiptoes and the shape of her tight bottom was captivating. She glanced a question over her shoulder to me one final time, and then called out to Mrs. Solomon and the other women, gathered just below our suite.

"I waited. I heard Mrs. Solomon's voice, louder than all the other women, and I saw Caroline nod and wave. I went to my suitcase, and then out through the glass doors, keeping away from the edge of the wall. I set one of the outdoor furniture chairs in place behind Caroline and sat behind her.

"No one could see me. I was sitting close behind Caroline. She asked Mrs. Solomon how her oldest son was doing at school. I reached between Caroline's legs and eased them apart with my hands. Caroline balked – something she was saying seemed to get stuck in the back of her throat – and then she finished the question, her voice becoming a little softer suddenly.

"Mrs. Solomon began to answer. Caroline was suddenly standing stiff with anticipation. She had her legs spread and I could feel the heat radiating from her pussy as I worked my fingers slowly up inside the soft flesh of her thigh. I felt her shudder. Her bottom clenched tight, and then relaxed. My hand drifted to the top of her other thigh, and the tips of my fingers grazed the swelling lips of her pussy. She flinched and went suddenly rigid. I heard her gasp, but she turned it into a laugh. Mrs. Solomon laughed along with her.

"I had packed the riding crop, the handcuffs and a dildo in the suitcase – all the props from the room upstairs. I had the dildo in my other hand. I rubbed the swollen bulb of it against Caroline's pussy and she flinched in sudden surprise and shock. She glanced over her shoulder at me – saw me behind her. I snapped at her to turn around and do as I had ordered her. Even under the color of her skin, I could see her face was flushed.

"She carried on the conversation with Mrs. Solomon again. She arched her back, and the firm rounded shape of her perfect butt was thrust back at me like an invitation. She wiggled her feet wider apart. Mrs. Solomon said something and Caroline nodded and tossed her head to flick hair from her face. It was a perfectly natural gesture, but I could see the tiny signs of her tension and excitement in the way she held herself. I massaged the cleft of her sex with the head of the dildo until it glistened with the wetness of her growing arousal.

"That would have been like torture to her, Jonah," Leticia muttered. "How long did this go on for?"

"About ten minutes," I guessed. "I was very slow and deliberate. Sometimes I would ease the first inch of the toy inside her pussy, and withdraw it again. The dildo never stopped moving. I used it to massage her clit and to smear her sexy juices all over her pussy until she was wet and trembling. She wasn't leaning on the wall anymore – she was clutching at it. Her entire lower body was tensing and then relaxing as the dildo hunted across the soft folds and the opening of her sex. Then the conversation with Mrs. Solomon suddenly faltered, and I snatched the dildo away as punishment and left her aching and straining with her body, rocking her hips and shifting her weight, trying to keep it pressed against her.

"When I had Caroline in a state of turmoil, I eased the dildo all the way inside her pussy and held it there. She made a low throaty moan of satisfaction, and she gently rolled her hips, like she was swaying from side to side. I held the base of the dildo with the palm of my hand between her spread legs so that the tips of my fingers were brushing against the sensitive nub of her clit. Caroline lowered her head and I saw she had her eyes closed, her lips parted. She was taking long deep breaths, as if the experience was something profoundly sensual that had spread from the center of her sex, out to every part of her aching body.

"I told her to say goodbye to the women gathered around the pool, and then I led her back inside our room.

"Caroline walked towards the bed. I took her arm and led her instead to a small two-seater sofa. I told her to lay back. She spread her legs wide and propped her head on the armrest. One long brown leg was draped across the back of the sofa so that her pussy was wide open for me. I knelt between her legs and drew my tongue slowly all the way up the lips of her pussy to the throbbing nub of her clit. Caroline hissed, and her hands reached for my head. Her eyes were screwed tightly shut and her mouth hung open. She was panting.

"I stopped suddenly. I didn't need to say a word. The message was in my eyes. Caroline's hands went to her side and bunched into fists. She clawed at the upholstery and dug her fingers into the cushions. I lowered my head slowly again. She felt my breath on her sex and she arched her back a little in anticipation. I made her wait for long torturous seconds – and then sucked her clit gently between my lips – and hummed."

"Hummed?"

I nodded. "It's like a dull vibrating sensation, especially if the man can generate the sound in the back of his throat and keep the sound a deep, low rumble," I explained. "It's a gentle way of stimulating a woman's most erotic places without too much pressure. Some women are very sensitive. This works – not for every woman – but more often than not."

Leticia flipped through several blank pages and made a separate note in the back of her book.

"How did Caroline react?"

"Humming against a woman's clit is like a gradual stimulation," I said. "It's a bit like how a high-pitched sound shatters a glass. The vibrations build up gradually, until they radiate out beyond the woman's clit, until her whole pussy starts to tingle. Caroline bit her lip and kept her eyes closed, concentrating. One of her hands reached for her breast and began to tease and pinch her nipple. I felt her slowly begin to grind her hips in tight circles and her breathing became hectic and agitated.

"I felt her clit hardening and seeming to grow between the soft press of my lips. I licked at the juices of her pussy, like a man dying from thirst.

"Caroline asked me if she could have an orgasm. I made her wait ten excruciating seconds, and then gave her my permission.

"Caroline went rigid, and her breath seized. There was a husky growl in her throat, and she clung to the edge of the sofa as if she might fall. She held her breath for long seconds. Her face twisted into a grimace of sweet torture – and then suddenly she exploded in a writhing tangle of arms and legs and groans of deep satisfaction."

Leticia stopped mid-sentence and threw her pen down. She brushed hair from her face and stared at me in confusion and frustration.

"Jonah, I don't understand this," she said. "I don't follow why you would go out of your way to give a submissive such as Caroline orgasms – I mean by making the effort to pleasure her. I thought BDSM was all about the man's pleasure, and the woman received her satisfaction from submitting," she said, and there was genuine passion in her voice as though this mattered and was important to her. "I thought it was more an emotional kind of satisfaction for the woman, not a physical thing like it is for the Master."

I stopped pacing. I stood still. For a long moment I said nothing – I just stared into Leticia's eyes, enjoying this new passionate side of her personality that I hadn't witnessed before.

"Leticia, do you remember the definition I gave you for *'do ut des'*?" I asked kindly.

She nodded.

"It means *'I give that you may give'*. It might as well be the slogan for healthy BDSM relationships. The lifestyle is not about some man standing over a woman and using her body simply to *take* his pleasure. Yes, sometimes, in some circumstances, that happens. But in all of my BDSM experiences, it has been about reciprocal giving. *I give pleasure*, so that *she will give back* to me. No relationship can last if it is one-sided. There are women who receive a great deal of emotional satisfaction from giving pleasure, and they are less interested in their own sexual needs, but the key here is the word 'give' – not 'take'. Sometimes a random BDSM scene might be just about the Master, but in any kind of an ongoing BDSM relationship, it is important that both the Master and the submissive are truly satisfied. Otherwise, it's not a relationship worth being in, is it?"

"No," Leticia agreed.

"Caroline was a highly sexual, erotic woman. Her satisfaction came in physical forms, not emotional. But there is more to it than that, Leticia," I explained. "For Masters like me, orgasm denial is an important punishment technique in the training process."

Leticia picked up her pen. "Should I write this down?"

I nodded. "If you want to fully understand, yes."

I prowled to the edges of the kitchen, moving in and out of the shadows as I began to pace again. "I don't believe in inflicting pain – especially on a woman. To me, pain is unworthy of a Master, and totally unnecessary. I know there are some submissives that are aroused by pain, but they're not the ones I have ever chosen to take on. For me, it is crucial that the submissive knows the rules and knows the consequences for disobedience. My preferred method of punishment is to deny her orgasms. Depending on the severity of the infraction, I might deny her for a day, a week... sometimes maybe longer. But the whole punishment system depends on one thing..." I left the sentence unfinished, the answer hanging in the air.

"She must have orgasms," Leticia said with slow realization.

I winked at her and smiled. "Precisely. If the submissive doesn't know how intense and overwhelming I can make her orgasms, then she doesn't appreciate what she stands to lose from disobeying me. If I give her orgasms, she fully appreciates what she might miss out on if she crosses the established lines. I find it works better than a riding crop, better than any other punishment."

Leticia nodded. "It makes good sense."

"So bringing Caroline to orgasm with my mouth on that sofa was more than about just pleasing her. It served many purposes."

"What happened after Caroline orgasmed?"

"She was like a rag doll," I said. "Her orgasm left her drained and satiated. I unbuckled my belt and went to where she lay. Her head was turned to the side, propped on the armrest of the sofa. My cock was hard. Caroline had her eyes closed, and her chest was still heaving as she caught her breath. I rubbed the hardness of my cock across her lips, and her mouth fell open obediently to me. I watched the swell of her breasts as she breathed, and held her mouth open for me to use.

"I was in no hurry. I enjoyed the feel of myself brushing across her wet tongue, and sliding deeper down her throat. Her eyes fluttered open and she stared up at me, her expression passive and willing. I covered her eyes with my hand, so that her focus became only the feel of my hardness between her lips."

"You covered her eyes with your hand?"

"Yes. Guys are all visual. Women are much more sensory. Their arousal comes from so many different stimuli. I wanted Caroline to concentrate on the hardness of my cock, and on the soft wet sounds as she sucked me – and the sounds of my breathing as I became more aroused."

"Why was that important?"

"Because I wanted Caroline to focus on me, and become aware of how I felt and the way I responded. I didn't want her to read my expression, I wanted her to read and understand my body, so that she would begin to know and recognize the signs, even in the darkness.

"I clenched my muscles and my cock leapt and pulsed and thickened within her mouth. Caroline made a soft sound of delight. I did it again, and her sound became one of hunger.

"I slid myself from between her lips and reached for Caroline's arm. She seemed to sense instinctively what I needed. She fell to her knees on the floor and bent herself over the sofa, parting her legs wide for me and resting her face on the cushion. She looked over her shoulder to me and her eyes were smoky.

"She was still wet from her orgasm. I entered her slowly, drawing out the moment and feeling every ripple and pulse of her body as it wrapped snugly around my shaft. Caroline closed her eyes again and moaned, the sound muffled by the sofa cushion. When I was all the way inside her, I began to move. I dragged my fingernails down her spine and her back arched in a slow voluptuous thrill. I tugged off her bikini top and reached around to cup one of her swaying breasts in the palm of my hand. Her flesh was warm, her nipple hard as a pebble. I squeezed and kneaded it gently as she began to rock her body in time with each thrust of my hips.

"I entangled my fingers in her hair and then suddenly thrust hard and urgently. Caroline groaned. I felt a mighty shudder ripple through her body and her bones seemed to soften with renewed desire."

Leticia got up suddenly from the kitchen table and tossed her head in a gesture I couldn't read. She breathed hard and hugged her arms tight around her body and shivered. My shirt she was wearing bunched and gaped around her breasts but she seemed not to notice.

"Something wrong?"

"It's just hot," Leticia said softly. There was a peculiar expression on her face. "I need to stretch my legs for a moment."

I stayed back, leaning against the kitchen counter, and watched Leticia move. Her steps were light and stealthy, bristling with some hidden tension. She stalked close to me and I reached out for her. She stopped and stared up into my face, her huge eyes startled. I brushed my finger across her cheek. She began to tremble.

"You are every bit as beautiful as Caroline, and much more than that in so many ways," I reassured her in a whisper. Leticia looked like she might cry. She was suddenly rigid. I put one hand gently on her shoulder. I could smell the scent of her perfume and an aroma like apples in her hair. Her eyes stayed locked onto mine. "And one day you are going to be an amazing journalist. Don't be in too much hurry, Leticia. For anything. You're still young. That's your problem. There is a lot of good and bad about life you still have to learn."

I pulled her gently towards me. Her eyes became urgent, grew even wider, but she came to me unresisting. I leaned in and kissed her on the forehead, and then stepped back before the last shreds of my control gave way, and my want and desire overwhelmed me again.

My hands were shaking slightly. I thrust them into my pockets.

It was late, and the atmosphere in the kitchen had suddenly become dangerous. I listened in the silence and heard rain still falling lightly outside.

"The worst of the storm seems to have finally passed," I said just a little too loudly for it to sound natural. "And your sweater should be dry by now..."

Leticia nodded numbly. There was a far-away look in her eyes for long seconds until the words finally registered and she glanced around, dull and unfocussed, as though she had forgotten where we were and why we were here.

"My notes..." she began. "They're not finished. Is there more to what happened between you and Caroline in the hotel?"

I was tempted to lie – but I didn't.

I nodded.

Leticia sat back down, and I went to the table and turned a chair around, sitting astride it so that the backrest was like a physical barrier between us. I folded my arms across the top of the chair and rested my chin on my forearms, brooding into the shadows beyond where Leticia sat waiting silently, with the notebook in her lap and her legs crossed.

"I drove my cock repeatedly into Caroline's pussy," I began again at last, "marveling at how perfectly our bodies seemed to fit together, and how in tune she seemed to be with my own needs. It was as though she could anticipate each thrust, and she used her body to amplify the sensations I could feel building within me.

"She began to make breathless little sounds of desire. I put my hands on her hips and demanded she tell me how it felt to submit her body to her Master – how it felt to give herself for my pleasure. Caroline snarled, like some ferocious wild lioness at the end of her tamer's whip, and the words tumbled from her in a litany of filthy erotic language that no lady would ever use. Her crude coarse words, and the tone she used, drove me feverishly towards the edge.

"I heard my breath rasping hoarse as sandpaper in my throat. At the last possible moment I reeled away, my chest wet with sweat, my heart thumping like a drum. Caroline turned round on her knees and took the length of me urgently into her mouth. I threw my head back and groaned at the ceiling as her lips wrapped tight around the head of my cock and the first pulse of my orgasm erupted across her tongue. She swallowed, drew a deep satisfied breath, and then took me into her mouth again until I was spent and exhausted and barely able to stand."

There was no more to the story. I leaned back on the seat of the chair and sighed. I sensed the first symptoms of a headache and shook my head as if that might actually help. It didn't.

Leticia continued to stare down at the page of her notebook long after she had finished writing. The silence in the kitchen was suddenly deafening.

She looked up at me at last, with a fragile expression on her face and her bottom lip trembling. "I think I might get my sweater and go home." She spoke like there was so much more she wanted to say, but wouldn't.

Leticia followed me to the top of the stairs. The door of the study was open. The fire had burned down to glowing coals so that the room was almost shrouded in total darkness. I waited at the threshold. Leticia drifted into the room and I saw the outline of her moving towards the leather sofa. I stared discreetly down the hall, and a moment later she was back by my side, wearing her sweater once more with my shirt in her hand. She offered it to me. "Thanks," she said.

I walked with her downstairs and into the foyer. I held the front door open. "Tomorrow?" she asked uncertainly.

"Of course," I smiled. "I'll call you."

I watched her to her little car. It started in a belch of grey smoke. The engine sputtered, then roared to life and Leticia drove out through the main gates and into the misting night.

I pushed the door closed and stood in the silence.

I held the shirt up and inhaled the lingering scent of her perfume.

* * *

When I knocked on Leticia's door it was just before three o'clock in the afternoon. She greeted me with a smile and stepped aside for me to enter.

The apartment looked somehow bigger and brighter. Leticia had thrown open all the drapes so that warm afternoon sunlight streamed into the living room. The window was open, and I could hear the muted sounds of the city drifting on the still air. Leticia was wearing a t-shirt and old jeans. I shrugged off my jacket and hung it over the back of a dining table chair.

I felt comfortable here. I felt comfortable with Leticia. Her smile was easy. I had spent the morning at a meeting in the heart of the city. I slipped the knot of my tie and unfastened the top button of my shirt, then set about rolling up my sleeves.

"Are you ready for a long afternoon?"

Leticia nodded. She had all of her notebooks stacked on the coffee table. Beside the books were loose pieces of paper. She picked up a sheaf of the pages and brought them to me.

"These are my editor's notes," she explained. "I've been on the phone with the office since before lunchtime. The boss is excited about the article, Jonah. He's keen to publish the first part of your story in next Saturday's edition."

I scanned the pages. Overshadowing the moment was the realization for us both that the interview was almost over. In a couple more days, my story would be told. I felt the pang of impending loss like a dull ache in my chest that I couldn't quite ignore. It was like a single dark cloud in a clear blue sky.

I handed the pages back, but the smile stayed firmly fixed on my face. "That's fantastic, Leticia," I said, and my enthusiasm was genuine. "I'm sure you will do a fine job."

She shrugged and suddenly became self-conscious. She made a pained face. "Well if I don't, it's my ass," she said. "My internship finishes soon. If this interview doesn't convince the editor I have what it takes, I'm afraid I might be on the bus back home."

I shook my head. "You've got nothing to worry about," I said. "I've read your work. You'll do fine."

"You read my work?"

I nodded. "Before you arrived that first day for the interview. I had some of the stories you wrote sent to me. I thought they were good."

She made a face. "Jonah, so far the most exciting story I have covered was the annual garden show. It's not exactly Pulitzer prize winning material."

"I saw your potential," I said. "I'm sure your editor does too."

We drifted into the kitchen. Leticia made coffee and I watched her as if she were some alchemist brewing a secret potion. She used the exact same ingredients I had the evening before, and yet somehow the coffee she made tasted fine.

"When we finished up last night, you had just told me about the time you spent with Caroline at the hotel," Leticia said. Her tone was conversational, like we were two old friends chatting. "Is there more you can tell me about your three years with Caroline – maybe a couple of other experiences that you remember?"

I set the coffee down on the counter. "Sure," I said. "But first I have a question for you. *'Do ut des'*."

Leticia had her hip resting against the edge of the bench top, her weight on one leg, so that the tight denim of her jeans folded into deep tantalizing creases below her zipper. The sleeves of the t-shirt were short, and her skin was lightly tanned and glowing with the freshness and luster of youthful good health. She tossed back her head, exposing the soft line of her neck to me, and her hair shook and shimmered.

She seemed to brace herself mentally, and then nodded. "Ask."

I had thought long and hard about this question. More than any other, this was the one I wished for her to answer.

"Do you actually like me, Leticia?"

She physically flinched, as though shaken, and her expression changed gradually over the course of several seconds.

"If it wasn't for this interview – if we had just met as a man and a woman, would I have been someone you would like?"

Leticia seemed to lean towards me, and then pull back. "Jonah, I admire you, more than you will ever know," she said softly, her eyes searching my face. "You're gallant, you're a gentleman, and you're definitely larger than life. Yes, I like you – you know that – *but I wouldn't want to be like you."*

I blinked. "Why not?"

Leticia smiled wistfully. "You're larger than life, Jonah. You fill a room and suffocate me. Your energy, your personality is like this big unstoppable force. You sweep people off their feet and draw them towards you like a comet. I… I could never be like that," Leticia said. "Most people could never be like that. The majority of us watch the world go by, and adapt to what life hands us, Jonah. But you're different. You can change your world. That seems like a wonderful gift, but I also think it's a heavy burden. Personally, I don't know how you do it."

Leticia lowered her head for a long moment, and I thought she had finished speaking. Then she lifted her face again and there was sudden regret and sadness in her eyes.

"If you hadn't pushed me away, I would be in your arms right now, Jonah. I wanted that. When you kissed me…" her voice broke off and when it came back one final time it was nothing more than a whisper. "Yes, I like you."

"I'm sorry I hurt you," I said. I meant it. I felt Leticia's body draw towards me, and then her cell phone rang, the sound shrill as an alarm in the intimate silence. Leticia sighed and stepped back, breaking the spell that seemed to have been cast upon us.

"See," she said wryly. "My phone rings – and now I am going to adapt to what life is about to hand me. If it had been your phone, Jonah, you probably would have been able to will it into silence."

I smiled into her eyes. "If it had been my phone, Leticia, I would have turned it off ten minutes ago."

She threw me a playful look over her shoulder and snatched up her phone from the table. I carried my coffee to the window and stared down at the city. Long meandering lines of traffic cluttered the streets, sunlight glinting off windshields as cars crawled through the crisscross of downtown intersections. I stared without really seeing until I heard Leticia finish her conversation and toss her cell onto the sofa.

"Problem?" I turned and asked.

"The office," Leticia sighed. She scraped her hands through her hair and stood with one hand on her hip. "They need the copy for the first part of your interview by Thursday. I've just lost a whole twenty-four hours of time to write and prepare."

"Is that critical?"

She nodded. "It is when you have no confidence in your ability, and you are about to write the article that could make your entire journalism career, yeah. It's kind of a big deal."

"Solution?"

"Start looking for another job," Leticia said, but she wasn't smiling. "Or find some way to turn back time."

I shook my head. "I don't like your choices," I said. "So how about option three? Why not make extra time."

"How?"

"We'll finish the interview today," I said. "If you're happy to put in long hours, we can wrap this up tonight. That would give you the extra time you need."

* * *

Leticia made herself comfortable on the sofa and I went and stood by the open window. She had a fresh notebook ready. Her legs were crossed, and she sat looking up at me with an air of expectation.

I felt sunlight on my back, warm through my shirt. "Caroline's biggest problem as a submissive was her discipline," I announced. "She was a very passionate, sexy woman, and she had a mind of her own. I have told you before that she was very beautiful and very intelligent. Sometimes her independence meant that training her to submit and obey presented its challenges.

"Orgasm denial became common in our relationship. Caroline couldn't quite find the line between retaining her own independence as a woman, and submitting to a Master. She would go for days, and sometimes even a week without an orgasm because she disobeyed me, or was ill-disciplined."

"And yet you regarded her as a good submissive?"

I nodded.

"How did you enforce the orgasm denial punishments? It must be based on a lot of trust."

"It is," I admitted. "It depends on the submissive being honest. There is no point in me punishing a woman by denying her orgasms if she breaks the rules by pleasuring herself. When we were having sex, I would turn the punishment into the most exquisite torturous agony she could possibly endure by getting her to the brink of exploding, and then backing off, being sure that after each session she was sexually aroused, but left frustrated. It was the very best way to encourage a submissive like Caroline to change her behavior."

"How did that work?" Leticia asked. "I don't quite follow."

I started to pace.

"It was normal for me to insist that all my submissives ask permission to orgasm," I said. "That way I had control of their releases, and could use that control to heighten their pleasure, or drive them crazy with desire and anticipation. Caroline was no different. Whenever we were having sex, she was required to ask my permission before being allowed to have an orgasm.

Leticia cut in. "And that is normal?"

"It's normal for me," I said. "I insist submissives ask permission before they come. I don't know about other Masters, but I imagine the practice is pretty common."

She made a note of that on a separate page of her book, and then flipped back to the page where she had left off. "And so you would use this punishment technique to keep Caroline on edge, right?"

"Right," I said. "I remember one particular session that was held in the upstairs room I showed you next to my bedroom. Caroline had been denied orgasms for a full week, and during those seven days I had used her for my own pleasure on several occasions, wickedly teasing her pussy as I fucked her, but never quite letting her come. For the first two days she endured, but as I said, she was naturally a highly sexual person. By the fifth day she was begging and pleading with me to allow her an orgasm – even if it was merely one she gave herself while I watched her. I said no. By the last day of the punishment she was on the brink of having a meltdown. For her, being denied an orgasm was like being denied chocolate, or oxygen.

"I told her to meet me in the upstairs room, and I was waiting for her when she arrived. She was bright and smiling. She glowed with excitement. She stood before me in black lace panties and bra, and heels. Her body was perfect; her skin was flawless, her breasts the perfect size and shape, her waist tiny, and her legs long and toned.

"She was trembling with suppressed excitement and there was a trace of a smile in her eyes. She looked up at me with hooded eyes and licked her lips.

"'I am ready to give my body to you, Master,' Caroline breathed demurely. I smiled at her. I asked her if she would be my good girl from now on. She nodded her head vigorously. I asked her if my good girl would obey all of her Master's instructions. Again, she nodded vigorously. I walked to the table in the middle of the room and stood there for several seconds. Every day for the past week I had taken Caroline as she stood bent over the table with her legs spread widely. Now, as I moved in the same way I had every day for the past week, she slipped her thumbs into the elastic of her panties and pulled them down.

"I asked her one last time if she promised to be my good girl, and she nodded again. I smiled my pleasure at her and she beamed back at me. 'You can suck my cock, today,' I said. 'I have no need for your pussy. I have decided you can make me come with your mouth.'

"Caroline froze for a second, and then shot me a disbelieving glare. The expression hung on her face for a couple of seconds before she realized I was watching her carefully. The look transformed to one of bewilderment.

"'It has been a week, Master,' she reminded me gently. 'I have gone for so long without an orgasm. I thought that today... that well... I would have earned my release.' I shook my head sadly, and told Caroline that she had indeed served her week-long punishment, but that didn't entitle her to an orgasm. It merely meant that she was no longer prevented from having an orgasm. I assured her that the next time I used her pussy for my pleasure, she would be allowed to come – but that I had decided the following week would be made up of several cock-sucking sessions. I might not want her pussy for some time.

"Caroline's expression became terrible. It was like watching the four seasons of a year, played out in her emotions. She went from smiling and radiant with expectation, to distant and detached, to icy cold, her lips pale and drawn into a thin bloodless line. Her eyes blazed with resentment – and then she made the mistake of openly questioning me. If she had a tail, it would have swished with agitation."

Leticia was furiously scribbling notes to keep up with me. I got tired of pacing back and forth, and did a circuit around the dining table while I waited for her to catch up.

"So what happened?" she asked at last.

"I ordered Caroline onto her knees," I said. "And I told her to open her mouth. She obeyed, but all of the vitality had gone from her. She was sullen and brooding. She had put make-up on before coming to the room. Her lips were red and glossy and full. I unbuckled my belt, stepped out of my jeans, and stood before her. She had her hands resting on her knees. I reached down and casually fondled one of her breasts, and then lifted it from the cup of her bra. I rolled the nipple between my thumb and forefinger and felt it harden to my touch. Caroline said nothing. I could hear her breathing, but it was a sound more like a simmer. She was angry, and that pleased me."

"Pleased you?"

"Absolutely," I said.
"Why?"
"Because an important lesson was being taught and learned, Leticia. A lesson that Caroline needed to understand about discipline. It gave me no pleasure to be mean. That wasn't the objective. I would have preferred if she had accepted my decision with the good grace I expect from my submissives, but she hadn't. I wasn't about to relent."
I stopped in the midst of the story and turned to glance out of the window for a moment. "Write this down." I said. "On a new page."
Leticia flicked through to the end of her book.
"To my way of thinking, a good Master is the iron fist within a velvet glove," I said. "The man needs to be firm and resolute. He needs to be confident and assured. He needs to be her rock: the one man in the world his submissive can turn to for advice, help, guidance and comfort. And he needs to be able to arouse and excite her. He needs to be able to keep her on edge and off balance. He needs to know her better than she knows herself – and he needs to be all these things to her without losing his honor, or destroying her dignity and independence. He needs to lift her up, Leticia, so that she becomes the person she wants to be, and then he needs to hold her there so she can never ever fall."
Leticia stared up at me and for a long time said nothing. She just stared at me.
Finally, I started to get uncomfortable. Leticia was gazing at me with a fixed, fascinated expression that was becoming unnerving. I said,

"Being a good Master, in my book, is much more than meets the eye, and it's much more than people outside of the lifestyle seem to really understand."

Leticia seemed to shudder, as though waking from a dream. Her eyes came into focus and grew wider. She blinked, and then stared down at her notes, reading back what I had said, silently mouthing each word.

I went on, and got back into the monotonous rhythm of pacing across the room.

"I slid my cock slowly across Caroline's lips and into her open mouth. Her lipstick smudged as she wrapped tight around the length of my shaft and I eased myself back and forth across her tongue. She stared up at me with her eyes fixed on mine, and let me take my pleasure.

"I reached down and tangled my hands in her hair. I held her head steady and began to thrust more deeply with my hips. Caroline's breathing became more feverish and ragged, but her body felt stiff and unwilling.

"I lost my patience at last. I withdrew my cock from her mouth and stalked across to the chair. I dragged it away from the table and sat. I glared at Caroline. I ordered her to bend over my lap."

"You did what?"

"I ordered her over my lap," I repeated, "and then I spanked her."

Leticia recoiled. "Are you serious?"

"Very," I said grimly. "Caroline came to me and she had tears welling up in her eyes. I told her to bend over my knee. She nodded and folded her body over mine so that her legs were stretched and parted out behind her, and she was supporting her weight on her extended arms, as if she were doing a push up. I felt the soft warm flesh of her breasts against the side of my thigh. I heard Caroline give a little grief-filled sob. I ignored her.

"I tugged the lace of her panties down her parted thighs and put one hand between her shoulder blades. I felt Caroline shudder. Then I cupped my hand and swatted one cheek of her bottom."

"Hard?" Leticia was fascinated. She had edged her body forward on the sofa and was leaning towards me.

"Of course not," I said. "I didn't want to hurt her. Being spanked is more a psychological punishment than a physical one. I smacked her bottom half-a-dozen times until her flesh was glowing a soft crimson red and I could feel the heat radiating up through my hand. Caroline was sobbing softly, her whole body tensed, anticipating the next smack.

"'Are you going to be a good girl from now on?' I demanded. Caroline sniffed away tears and assured me she would. She promised she had learned her lesson. I slid my palm across the swell of her butt and then dipped my hand down into the molten heat between her parted thighs.

"She was wet, and her arousal had coated the lips of her pussy so that two of my fingers eased inside her. Caroline's back seemed to heave. I felt her body clench tight to grip at me, and I left my fingers resting inside her pussy while she tried desperately to wriggle herself back on my hand to feel my touch more deeply. I felt her body rubbing against the hardness of my cock. I told Caroline to remain still. She flinched, and then went limp across my knee. I withdrew my fingers and used them to strum across the swollen bud of her clit.

"Caroline moaned. It was a sound I knew well. She was creeping towards the point where she would be on the brink of coming. The sound was deep in the back of her throat, breathless and somehow urgent. I kept playing my fingers across her clit in a steady rhythm. A few moments later she asked me in a timid voice if she had my permission to orgasm."

"And...?" Leticia prompted.

"I told her she could – but that she would have to do it herself. I told her to lie across the table and spread her legs. I wanted to watch her. Caroline squealed. The idea of pleasuring herself while I watched appealed to her exhibitionist side. She kissed me impulsively and settled herself on her back, legs splayed wide apart so that I could see the wet open lips of her sex from where I sat.

"My cock was still hard. Caroline raised her head and looked down through the jutting rise of her breasts and between her parted thighs at me. She had a soft, secret smile on her lips. Once she was assured I was watching, she laid back on the tabletop and stretched out. Her hand snaked down between her legs and she coated the tips of her fingers with her own wet arousal. I watched her with interest. I watched the ways she touched herself, and how she cupped and teased her breasts with her free hand. I listened to the sound of her breathing and the way her hips began to undulate as she sped towards her release. She became frantic. Her breathing stopped, then came again in great gulps. She tilted her pelvis and then arched her back.

"And then she orgasmed."

I stared off into space for a long moment, looking at the wall opposite but not really seeing it. I heard Leticia's voice, seeming to come from far away.

"What are you thinking about?" she asked.

I blinked. "I was wondering if you had any whisky."

Leticia shook her head. "Sorry. I have water."

"That will do." I went to the kitchen, found a glass in a cupboard and filled it with tap water. As a rule I never drank the stuff. Fish have sex in water… think about that…

Leticia took a plastic jug of water from inside the refrigerator door and filled another glass. She sipped at it.

"Did it bother you when Caroline started to cry as you put her over your knee to be spanked, Jonah?" Leticia asked softly. "You don't seem to be the kind of man who would take any pleasure from seeing a woman in tears."

I smiled, kind of. "In normal circumstances it kills me to see a woman cry," I admitted. "I don't think there is anything sadder in the world. In normal circumstances. But this wasn't a normal circumstance. Caroline was just using a woman's first defense to try to manipulate me and get her way."

Leticia tensed, suddenly wary. "A woman's first defense? That is going to need some explaining.

What do you mean by that?" she was instinctively guarded.

"Women have three defenses they use against a man to get their way," I said. "The first defense is tears. The second defense is abuse, and the third defense is violence. If they cry, and still cannot get what they want, they become abusive – and if that doesn't work, they become violent, or threaten violence. They throw plates, or threaten to throw things." I shrugged.

"You sound sexist."

I shrugged again.

"So, are you speaking as an expert, Mr. Noble?" Leticia's tone had turned decidedly frosty.

"No," I admitted. "I'm merely speaking as a man who has had enough arguments to recognize the pattern."

Leticia said nothing for a long moment, and then shook her head as though I confounded her. "You're such a contradiction, Jonah Noble," she said softly. "You're capable of expressing the most beautiful, profound ideas one moment, and the next, you're... you're a typical man."

I changed the subject. "Are you hungry?"

Leticia shrugged. "I could eat."

"There's a quaint little pizza place on Sixth Street. Do you know it?"

She nodded.

"I feel like pizza," I said. "It will be my treat."

* * *

'Dino's' was one of those authentic-looking Italian pizza places that was actually run by a Chinese couple. A red, green and white awning that stretched out over the sidewalk shaded the shop front, and there were empty wine bottles on shelves displayed in the windows.

I pushed open the door and held it for Leticia. A little bell attached to the frame tinkled, and an elderly Chinese gentleman came from a back room. He had an apron tied around his waist and a mouth full of gold teeth. He smiled at me. I smiled at him. He smiled at Leticia, and then we were shown to a booth in a gloomy corner at the back of the restaurant.

The menu was a folded card, wedged upright on the table between the sugar bowl and a ketchup bottle. I handed it to Leticia.

"Your choice," I said.

She ordered pizza. The restaurant was quiet – it was too late for the long lunch crowd to still be eating, and too early for the after work crowd. We stared out through the windows watching the world go by in a dull haze of smog and noise, until the pizza finally arrived on a wide wooden chopping board.

"What do you like to do in your spare time?" I asked. It wasn't the most probing question I had ever asked a woman, but it felt a little like we were taking time out.

"I read," Leticia said. She had a slice of pizza balanced delicately in one hand and a paper napkin in the other. "I like to read recipe books. I love cooking. What about you?"

I shrugged. “I don’t get a lot of spare time,” I said, “but when I do I like to read too. I have an interest in the fighter pilots and planes that flew during the First World War.”

Leticia made a face like she was surprised. “That’s kind of random,” she said.

Was it? I didn’t know.

“My father had a collection of miniature models at the old estate. I brought them with me. They’re in my office,” I explained.

Leticia nodded. “I saw them,” she said. “I just didn’t figure they were of particular importance to you. Why the fascination?”

“I admire the bravery of those men,” I said. “They were called the ‘knights of the air’. They fought to the death in planes made from wood and canvas, but managed to remain chivalrous and honorable in the most grueling of circumstances. Their heroism in the face of impossible adversity is pretty inspirational.”

I heard the bell above the door ring and glanced over my shoulder. A man and a woman with a couple of young children in tow were waiting to be shown to a table. We finished our pizza and I left two twenty dollar bills on the counter.

We walked slowly back through the city, our bodies close but never quite touching. Leticia leaned in to me whenever she spoke, and clutched at my arm as we crossed the street. The sun was setting on the horizon as we stepped in through the front door of her apartment – golden light spilled through the window in a long rectangular patch across the carpet and tinted the color of the walls. Leticia drew the heavy drapes and suddenly everything became gloomy. She switched on a couple of lamps and settled herself back on the sofa.

"Did you ever lose control with Caroline, Jonah?" Leticia asked. "She was clearly a feisty, independent woman. Surely there must have been times when you lost your temper with her."

"Never."

"Not even during sex, or when punishing her?"

"Never," I said again.

Leticia arched a questioning eyebrow.

"Leticia there were certainly times with Caroline where the sex we shared was aggressive – times when I took her for my pleasure and the sex-play was more physical. But it was all an act. It was all part of the scene we were involved in. There is no excuse for a man to become violent with a woman, and even in the most passionate moments with Caroline, she knew that everything happening was part of the moment, not part of my personality."

"How do you do that? How do you keep your control?"

I had never considered the question. I thought for a moment. "Discipline, I guess. And always remembering that the person you are with is in your care, and is relying on you to keep them safe."

"So how do you create those tempestuous, lust-filled moments without breaching your commitment to keep the woman you are with safe?"

I looked at Leticia with surprise. "Tempestuous?"

She smiled. "It's called a vocabulary."

I smiled back, and started to pace.

"More than anything else, every woman in the world wants to feel desirable, and desired," I said. "Caroline was no different. She was sexy, she was smart, and she was confident, but she was also a woman, and every woman I have known comes with a suitcase full of insecurities. And although every woman's suitcase is different, one thing always remains common – they want to know that they are attractive, even if it is only to the man in their life.

"Caroline needed that same reassurance, but it's a little different in a BDSM relationship. So much of what happens sexually is structured and arranged. For instance I would summon a submissive to kneel before me and suck my cock, or I would order her to remove her panties and bend over the edge of the table, and the woman would dutifully obey my instructions. Punishments, training sessions – everything tends to flow along organized lines.

"I found the best way to demonstrate to Caroline that she was desirable was to throw the rule book out once in a while, and simply act spontaneously."

"But not because you felt spontaneous?"

"No. That's how I always remain in control. I *acted* spontaneous for Caroline's sake."

Leticia wrote everything down, but I could see she didn't understand. It was like I was explaining English to a foreigner.

"One of my standing rules for submissives is that they are not permitted to wear panties when they are in the house, nor are they permitted to wear a bra. Under their clothes they are to be naked and available, and their pussy must always be shaved," I explained. "Each Master you speak to will have different rules. Those were some of mine."

"Can I ask what the reasoning is behind your rules?"

I smiled. "Anticipation," I said the magic word, "but also because I like my submissives to feel exposed and accessible. Making them go without underwear, gives them the sense that at any moment, their bodies might be used for giving pleasure."

Leticia bent over her notebook for a moment and I waited patiently until she was paying attention again, ready to go on.

"So whenever Caroline was nearby, she was always available to me. One afternoon I was in my office. The door was open. Caroline had just come back from the local gym. She walked past my door and glanced inside. She saw me at my desk and stopped. She was sweating. Her face was flushed red with exertion, and her skin glistened with a healthy glowing sheen. She lowered her head and stood perfectly still while my eyes roamed over her body. She was wearing a sports bra under her top and those tight black leotard things women wear when they work out. The clothes hugged her figure like a second skin.

"I asked her where she was going. She told me she needed to shower. I told her to be quick. I had use for her.

"I heard Caroline heading down the hall, and then a few moments later I heard the hiss of the shower. I waited five minutes and then got up from my desk – the work could wait. I went to the bathroom and pushed open the door. Clouds of steam swirled in the air. I pushed the door closed behind me. Behind the translucent glass of the shower stall I could see Caroline as a blurred silhouette.

"She saw me standing, watching her. I told her to turn off the shower. I told her I wanted her right then. I told her I couldn't wait even another minute.

"She came from the shower all glossy and wet, her hair hanging down her back, her body scrubbed and glowing.

"I reached for her. There was a possessive, primal growl in my throat. Caroline's eyes grew wide. For an instant alarm registered in her expression – but not with concern for her safety. It was a raw, instinctive look. A hunted look.

"I seized her arm and held it behind her back. Caroline gasped. I pulled her body back against mine so she could feel the hardness of my cock through my pants. I wrapped my other hand firmly around her throat and I hissed in her ear."

"What did you say?" Leticia asked with sudden interest.

"I told her I wanted her pussy. I told her that the sight of her, and the thought of her tight body bent before me, had sparked my need. I told her that the way she walked was pure sex in motion, and that I had to have her. I couldn't wait."

"But you could have, right?"

"Of course!" I said.

"It made no difference to me whether I took Caroline in the bathroom, in the play room, or the bedroom. But it mattered to her. Not only that, the manner I took her mattered. I wanted her to feel like she was incredible – that she turned me on so much I couldn't deny my instincts. I wanted her to feel ravaged and desired and lusted after. That's how I kept everything under control, Leticia. That's how my submissives were always safe and cared for – because even the most spontaneous moments were planned – even if the women never realized it."

Leticia was smiling secretly to herself as she made notes. She looked up at me again and tossed her head to flick hair from her eyes. "You're very clever, Jonah," she said simply. "You've thought this all out, haven't you?"

I dismissed her praise with a shrug of my shoulders. "I hate surprises," I said. "And I like to be in control."

"Do you feel the sex in the bathroom that day was different because of the way it occurred?"

"Absolutely," I said. "It didn't alter the intensity of my orgasm, or change the experience for me, but it tilted Caroline's world a little off its axis. I hoisted her onto the marble vanity, and dragged her forward until she was perched on the edge. She leaned back against the cold glass of the big bathroom mirror and I scooped her legs up and held them wide open with my hands beneath her knees. I told her to unzip my pants. She unfastened my belt and pulled my cock out through the opening in my clothes. She made a tremulous sound in the back of her throat and then groaned softly. My cock was hard and hot, too thick for her fingers to encompass entirely. She stroked me and I clenched my muscles, feeling my length leap and swell in her hand. Caroline guided me into her – she was wet and wanton with her own arousal, and I came up onto my toes and slid all the way inside her in a single powerful thrust. Caroline thrashed her head from side to side and I bucked my hips hard against her body. She threw her arms around my neck and clung to me like we were riding a wild storm. She cried out, and her body lunged forward against me. I felt the hard rub of her nipples against my chest and I bit at her neck and snarled.

"The sound of our bodies crashing together was loud above the noise of our ragged gasps. It was intense and explosive: a raw, lust-filled moment that was more than merely sex.

"We came together. I felt myself release deep within her and an instant later, Caroline's body seemed to heave and undulate. She groaned, and all the air seemed to be sucked from her lungs. Her mouth fell open in a breathless 'O' as a crashing orgasm rocked her."

I rubbed my eyes, and yawned. I was suddenly very tired.

"Every man should make the effort occasionally to throw the rule book out," I said. "It doesn't matter if the relationship is BDSM or vanilla – every man should go out of his way to make the woman in his world feel desired and wanted. It's worth the effort and planning to occasionally appear spontaneous."

I played those contradicting words back in my head to make sure the sentence made sense. Leticia did the same. I saw her silently reading the passage back to herself and then nod.

"Is that little gem of relationship wisdom in the Jonah Noble big book of rules?" she asked playfully.

I nodded. "Page sixteen."

For a long while I prowled restlessly in the shadows, hunting through my memories and discarding each one until I realized I had said enough. There was nothing more to say.

My story had been told.

I closed my eyes and sighed, not with any great relief, but with a sense of finality. And then Leticia asked the one question I had avoided for so long...

"What happened with Caroline six months ago, Jonah?" Leticia asked. "Why did your relationship end?"

I froze.

The smile slid from my face, and I felt ice spread slowly through my veins. "I decided to end Caroline's training," I said hoarsely. "It was for the best."

"Can you tell me why?"

"No." I said.

Leticia saw the look in my eyes, and sensed there was darkness and despair below the surface. "You don't want to talk about it?"

“I will not talk about it,” I said bleakly. “It’s the one question I will not answer.”

The atmosphere in the room turned brittle and cold – the air between us seemed suddenly to crackle. I paced in the shadows beyond the reach of the lamplight for long minutes until I felt the tension seep from my shoulders and my dark mood slowly drifting away. “Any other questions?”

Leticia cleared her throat, perhaps startled and made wary by my abrupt reaction. Her uncertain hesitation dragged on for long moments.

“Ask,” I demanded. I saw her flinch, and then nod her head.

“Do you have any photos of the women we have talked about?” The words came out in a breathless rush.

I had to think. “Not Claire,” I said emphatically. I knew that for a fact. “Maybe Sherry… and I definitely have some of Caroline. Why?”

Leticia shrugged. “I’d like to see them. I’d like to put faces to the names of these women that had such an affect on your life.”

I felt myself stiffen. “Leticia, the privacy of these ladies will be protected at all cost,” the hard edge returned to my voice. “No images of them will be used in your article.”

She shook her head. “Oh, I understand that, Jonah. I don’t want them for publication. I would never do that. I just wanted to see the people I was writing about.”

I relaxed a little, nodded slowly. “I think I can find some for you.”

“And your father?”

I frowned. "Leticia, you must have a million photos of my father in your newspaper files."

She nodded. "Yes, but I was hoping you might have one of you and him together – a private family photo that you would release for publication. One way or another, Jonah, he had an influence on the man you are today."

I hesitated, and then sighed. "When do you want them?"

"As soon as possible. Could I come by and pick them up in the morning?"

"Sure – but only the photo of my father and I will be used in conjunction with the article. Agreed?"

She held out her hand and we shook. She was smiling. "Agreed," she said.

I walked out into the warm night, and stood on the sidewalk for long seconds, feeling suddenly lost. It was over. The interview was finished, and with it went my reason for sharing time with Leticia.

I wondered if I would ever see her again after she came to the house tomorrow.

* * *

I came down the stairs in a somber, empty mood. My footsteps sounded hollow, and there was a dull ache of remorse behind my eyes – a sense of loss that seemed to haunt me like a shadow. The morning was bright and sunny. I could hear Mrs. Hortez in the kitchen finishing up with the breakfast dishes. I ambled idly through the house as though I was a stranger – as though all the purpose and energy had been drained from me. Bright shafts of sunlight lanced through the windows, painting patches on the floor. I wandered down the hall towards the back of the house and pushed open the door.

She was waiting for me. She turned with an expectant smile on her face.

Morning sunlight streamed in through the big windows, but despite that, Trigg's room seemed somehow colder than the rest of the house.

I said nothing. I stood in the doorway for long seconds and then lay down and stretched out on her big bed. I stared up at the ceiling, aware that she was drifting around the room on the edge of my vision. She was humming softly to herself.

"What time is it?" I asked quietly.

"Just after ten," Trigg answered in a whisper.

"Leticia will be here soon," I said. "We need to be quick. I don't want her to see us together. What did you want me for?"

She came to the side of the bed and stooped over me. She was smiling. She brushed hair away from her face. Her eyes were big and bright.

"There's plenty of time, Jonah," she said softly. "I just want you to relax. Don't think about Leticia. Try to clear your mind. There are some things I need you to see. It will only take a minute."

I heard Trigg walk slowly away towards the door and close it. When she came back to the side of the bed, she was holding an envelope out towards me, clutched in her long delicate fingers. She placed it on my chest and stood waiting.

"It's just some standard reports," she said.

"Good news or bad?" I asked impatiently. I was keen to be away from her room.

"Good. Nothing has changed…"

I reached for the envelope and as I did, I turned my head a little and caught a glimpse of Trigg's wristwatch. For an instant nothing made sense and then I frowned suddenly and sat up in alarm. An ice-cold dagger of dread stabbed at my heart. I felt the blood drain away from my face.

"Jesus!"

It was ten thirty five.

I threw the envelope down unopened and swung my feet off the bed. I shot Trigg a venomous glare. She recoiled away from me. I reached for the door as the enormity of her sabotage and betrayal finally began to overwhelm me. I threw the door wide open, and came from the room with a rising sense of outrage.

There was noise.

The front door slammed.

I spun round towards the sound.

Leticia was standing in the foyer. She was smiling brightly.

She saw me. She frowned. She shook her head slowly, like nothing made sense.

Then she saw Trigg in the doorway of her bedroom. Leticia's eyes flew wide and her mouth fell open as if she were in some terrible agony.

I glanced back over my shoulder. Trigg was looking past me towards Leticia. Trigg had a possessive complacent smile on her face. I locked my eyes with hers and her expression changed, burning with vindictive malevolence. It lasted for only a second – so fleeting that perhaps it might never have even been – if I hadn't seen it for myself.

"I had to," Trigg said. "I couldn't let this go on, Jonah."

Fury blinded me. I could hear the thump of my blood pounding at my temples.

By the time I turned back, Leticia's expression seemed to have crumbled.

"You're sleeping with Trigg?"

I went to her urgently. "Leticia! God, let me explain." I reached out for her. She stared as though she didn't recognize me. I took her arm, and suddenly she flew at me, wailing in despair, her arms flailing so that her nails raked bloody lines down my cheek and across my nose.

"I hate you!" she shrieked. "You lied to me. It's all been a lie!" She clawed for my eyes, vicious and wounded. I swung my head aside and then trapped her wrists.

"You told me there could be no future for us, Jonah. You told me that. And now I find it's because you're with Trigg. Why couldn't you tell me?" she moaned. There was heart-broken pain on her face. "Why couldn't you just tell me you were in love with her?"

She struggled and lashed out at me. I wrapped my arms around her waist and pinned her against me. I could feel the rigid unyielding tension in her body, and see her face slickened with tears.

I looked over her head and shot a withering glare at Trigg.

"You call this ethical?"

"No. I call it moral," Trigg's voice was imploring. "I had to do it, Jonah. This has gone on for too long. Can't you see that?"

I snarled at her, blazing with rage. "Get out!" I shouted. "Get the fuck out of this house, Trigg, and never come back!"

Trigg stood, rooted to the spot. She wrung her hands and then slowly began to shake. Tears welled in her eyes, and then her whole body began to shudder.

I grabbed at Leticia's arms, bracing them to her side and held her away from me.

"It's not how it seems, Leticia," I said, shaking her urgently. She wouldn't look at me. She was crying as though her broken heart would never mend. Tears streamed down her cheeks and dripped from her chin. I shook her again and shouted. "It's not how it looks! Trigg isn't my lover. She's my doctor."

The word echoed in the silence, seeming to hang in the air for long dreadful seconds.

"Trigg is my doctor," I said again, this time more gently, this time with my voice made husky by emotion. "She has been living here for the past six months – because I'm dying."

Leticia froze, and then faltered. She went suddenly soft within my arms. Her outrage turned slowly to confusion, to shock and then finally her face was a dreadful mask of tragedy. She shook her head slowly in disbelief. I nodded sadly.

"No..." Leticia moaned. She turned to Trigg.

"He has a year, maybe two," Trigg said softly.

"Are you sure?"

Trigg blinked. "Nothing can be certain..."

I let go of Leticia's arms. She swayed on her feet, reeling. I touched lightly at the side of my head. "I have a tumor," I said. "It's inoperable," and my voice became choked. I opened my arms and she came into them, and I held her tight against my chest. We clung to each other like two drowning people in a storm. "It's the only thing that kept us apart, Leticia, I swear to you," I muttered. "I wanted to love you so badly..." and then there was just the sound of her crying for a very long time while I held her and we rocked gently together.

My despair came in relentless waves, pounding at me, and then receding, until, finally, I broke our embrace and stared down into Leticia's eyes.

"It's the answer to the question you asked last night," I said softly. "It's the reason my relationship with Caroline ended. When I found out I was dying, I sent her away. And it's the same reason I fought so hard to keep you away."

For a long time we stood in total silence. It took me several minutes to push aside the pain of unhealed wounds, and terrible sadness. I saw images of Caroline's face again, the anguish in her features, the tears that seemed might drown her...

Sometimes doing the right thing can feel so very wrong.

I stared up at the ceiling, then closed my eyes and took a deep breath.

I opened my eyes again, and saw the same agony in this young woman's face. The pain I had tried so hard to keep secret and avoid was torn across her features.

"I've been getting migraines for the past year, and moments where I forget what I was just talking about," I explained quietly. "Then six months ago I had a seizure, Leticia. That's why Trigg moved in. She's been monitoring my medication, and going with me to the hospital for the MRI's." I made a brave attempt to smile, but it slid off my face. "And that's why I wanted you to write my story, and why it had to be done now. Because I don't know how much longer I have to live."

"Isn't there an operation?" Leticia asked. She was sobbing, and her lips trembled with the strength of her appeal.

I shook my head. "There is no operation. Trigg has been here since I sent Caroline away. She's monitoring the growth of the tumor. There's nothing that can be done."

Leticia shook her head with sudden defiance and disbelief. "So you're giving up on life?" she sounded appalled.

"No!" I said. "I'm going to fight this, Leticia. I'm going to fight with every ounce of energy and determination I have. I'm going to fight to the death – but it's *my* fight. It's *my* war. I won't have your heart broken as collateral damage."

"So you'll die alone?"

"I'll die fighting. Alone."

"But Jonah, I can – "

I shook my head. "No."

She struggled in my arms. "But I want to."

"No. Leticia, please. Just leave. Go now. Walk out that door, publish your newspaper article and forget me."

I let her go. My arms fell heavily to my side. She stood there for long agonizing moments wrenched to pieces.

"Please…" I said.

Leticia turned for the door. She moved in a daze. Her feet shuffled across the cold tiles. I watched her walk down the steps. I blinked. I felt tears scalding my eyes and my determination wavered. I felt a vast desolation crush down upon me, so that I wanted to cry out to her in my anguish to come back.

But I couldn't.

She got to the side of her car and then broke down sobbing. Her whole body shook, as though the pain would crush her. Her shoulders slumped, and she gave a low moan of such despair and shattered agony that I felt the deep raw ache of my heart breaking for her.

I closed the door slowly, and my world turned dark and cold.

* * * * *

That's my story so far.

As I sit here at my desk and write these words, the rain is falling outside my window. It's now been twenty-seven days since that terrible morning when I said goodbye to Leticia, and it seems like it has rained every single day.

The article was published in three parts, and some of the bigger newspapers around the country picked up the story. I'm glad about that.

And I have a new doctor. He's an older guy. He looks a little bit like Robert De Niro. He's upbeat and optimistic – good qualities to have in a doctor when you're facing death.

I don't know what lies ahead. I don't know what the future holds or even how much future there is for me.

But I'm alone, and I'm desperately lonely.

I miss Leticia. I had waited all my life to find that girl – and she came too late for me to love.

Printed in Great Britain
by Amazon.co.uk, Ltd.,
Marston Gate.